Acquainted With Butterflies

A Collection of Short Stories, Personal Essays & Poetry

J.C. Wing

This is a work of fiction. All characters, organizations and events portrayed in this collection are either products of the author's imagination or are used fictitiously.

Other Books
by
J.C. Wing

The Color of Thunder

The Gannon Family Series
Alabama Skye
A Skye Full of Stars
A Warm Winter Skye

Goddess of Tornado Alley Series
Goddess of Tornado Alley
Dead Beat Dates & Deities
Brides, Beasts & Baklava

Perfectly Unique: Missing Pieces Anthology
(for Autism Speaks)
The Key

Sean -
Thanks for being
such a wonderful,
important part of
my life.
Love,
JC Wing

Acknowledgements

Thanks to The Writing Challenge Warriors:
This collection would never have come to be had it not been for **A.K. Lawrence**. It's totally her fault ... and I'm so glad I said yes when she asked me if I wanted to take part in that month-long writing challenge. I thank her and those other authors who decided to join us, and who helped us make that thirty days last nearly half a year. **Randy Brown** and **Carol Cassada** wrote with us every day, and together we became The Writing Challenge Warriors. I thank those who went along for at least part of the ride, too. **Jennifer Sivec, Samantha Soccorso** and **Stephanie Kepke**. It was fun writing with you all.

Thanks to my beta reading team:
I've got quite a group assembled now, and I'm so very grateful to each and every one of you. I appreciate your ongoing enthusiasm, your feedback and your continued support. **A.K. Lawrence, Samantha Soccorso, Linda Thompson, Jennifer Bleyle, Lynn Hill, MaryAnn Schaefer, Tracy H. Gilmore, Katherine Klimoski, Erin Wolf, Randy Brown** and **James Lockwood**. Much love and gratitude to you guys!

Thanks to my home team:
They know how much writing means to me, and I get never-ending support and love from them. **Steven, Maya** and **Scott**, I'm lucky to have you.

And to my mom, Linda Thompson ...
... thanks for buying me all that typewriter ribbon all those years ago. Little did you know back then how this was all gonna shake out. You're the only other person who can possibly understand some of the more personal things I've written in the following pages. Thank you for not telling me I shouldn't—even if you really wanted to. I'm glad to have you with me on this journey.

Letter from the Author

Back in 2012, shortly before I published my first novel, I began blogging. I thought it would be a good way for me to advertise my books and to share all the thoughts and feelings I had throughout the writing and publishing process. It was, and I'm glad I started it. My blog was titled J.C. Wing—Author. Short, simple and to the point. I was so overwhelmed at the time by being a newbie in the book world that this was all the extra creativity I could muster.

About a year later, I changed the name of my blog to J.C. Wing and the Goddess. I didn't explain the name change, and no one asked. Quite honestly, I didn't have more than a handful of followers, and if any of them noticed the change, none of them thought to mention it. I was basically using the blog as a brain dump. I wasn't concerned with traffic, and I continued to post—although sporadically—simply because I enjoyed doing so.

In July 2016, A.K. Lawrence, a good friend and fellow author, asked me to join her on a thirty-day writing challenge. I'd never posted anything on a daily basis, but it sounded like fun. It was. So much so, in fact, that after that first thirty days was over, we found another challenge to tackle. We even started a Facebook group called Writing Challenge Warriors and had a few other loyal bloggers writing with us. We wrote daily through the end of the year, then weekly as we began 2017. When we decided to take a break, I'd written a total of 143 posts, and J.C. Wing and the Goddess had become much more than just a brain dump for me. (Incidentally, the release of Dead Beat Dates & Deities, the first book in the Goddess of Tornado Alley series cleared up any questions those quiet followers might have had about that name change my blog had undergone years earlier.)

Many of the prompts for our daily challenges urged me to share incredibly personal stories. Many of those were difficult for me because I chose to let down my guard and write honestly. I've included a few of those here in this collection, though most of the articles are works of fiction. I've added in a sprinkling of poetry. I don't write much of that now—unless the limericks I penned for Brides, Beasts & Baklava count—but during my middle school, high school and early adult years, I used this form of expression in abundance. You don't know how lucky you are that I've chosen to be selective about which poems made the final cut. You're welcome.

Until I took part in this series of challenges, I hadn't written many short stories. Within a few months, I had authored quite a few. Those stories are what I wanted to share most in Acquainted with Butterflies. Some of them are funny, some of them hold a bit of mystery, and a few of them are on the romantic side. A Day in Paris is a countdown story, beginning with the number ten and ending at number one, and In the Pursuit of Spring shows just how dramatic and over the top a teenage girl's imagination can be. One of the prompts asked us to modernize our favorite fairy tale. I chose The Nutcracker and the Mouse King, written by E.T.A. Hoffmann. My version, The Nutcracker and the Cheeseball, is much lighter and much funnier than the original. A couple of short stories that came from this six months of daily blog writing are absent because they've grown into full length novel ideas. Writing is an adventure, and ideas pop up all the time. My stories tend to linger inside my head, and there are a few of them included in the following pages that may also become much longer pieces in the future.

I hope you enjoy this collection. I invite you to come and hang out with me and the goddess on my blog. You never know what we might come up with next.

J.C. Wing
www.jcwingandthegoddess@blogspot.com

"Perhaps the butterfly is proof
that you can go through
a great deal of darkness
and still become
something beautiful."

Beau Taplin

"Butterflies can't see their wings.
They can't see how truly beautiful they are,
but everyone else can.
People are like that as well."

Naya Rivera

"I've always loved butterflies
because they remind us
that it's never too late
to transform ourselves."

Drew Barrymore

Silver Seas

Shining stars glimmer on distant waves
The glistening water
runs along the beach
and then chases itself back.
The sand lies in mounds …
and the castles fall slowly
wet and wounded,
they lie ruined
The seagulls fly
in the cool, moist air
shrill screams,
then silence
The moonlight casts a blue haze
over the land
Things seem magical,
yet cold
The breeze is soft
and the air is cool
The mood is quiet
The star filled sky is like
a crown of dark blue
filled with jewels
All alone,
a feeling of ownership takes place
The ocean becomes a palace
and I, its queen

2/3/86

Artist at Work

Paige had been missing for more than three weeks. The last time anyone saw her smiling face had been at the assembly on the first day of school. It seemed that no one, including Drew, knew where she had gone.

Out of the nearly four hundred kids that called the Winston School campus home, Paige was Drew's favorite. She was one of his best friends and his first real crush, but he would never admit it to anyone. The two of them hadn't spent any time together over the break, but there had been several emails and texts, and Paige regularly commented on the things he'd added to his social media accounts.

He followed her, too, and knew she had been quite a bit more adventurous throughout the summer months than he had been. Her family lived in Raleigh, but according to her posts on Instagram, she hadn't spent much time there. He'd seen pictures of her on the beach and at every single lighthouse that stood sentry along the Outer Banks.

Drew hadn't done much outside of Asheville over the summer. G-Ma, not a big traveler to begin with, was getting up there in years. She hadn't been feeling well since falling ill earlier in the spring, so the two of them stuck even closer to home than usual. It turns out that pneumonia is a hard thing to bounce back from when you're in your seventies.

It seemed to Drew that G-Ma had always been old, but age was a strange concept to a kid still too young to drive. His parents hadn't been around for a long time. He'd never met his dad and had no idea where the man had ended up. His mom? She was a different story. He knew exactly where to find her. She was buried near a marble angel statue in the Asheville cemetery and had been since Drew was four. His memories of her were hazy. At least none of them were bad.

At the beginning of sixth grade, Drew had become a boarder at Winston. The drive between G-Ma's house and the front gates took less than fifteen minutes, but the two places felt like worlds apart.

G-Ma was great. She was kind and had a wicked sense of humor. The two of them shared a good and comfortable relationship, and Drew couldn't remember a time in his life that she hadn't been a part of. When she mentioned one day at breakfast the fact that she'd been doing some research on the school, Drew knew it wasn't because she'd grown tired of his company.

She wanted him to have an adventurous life, one that went beyond making small talk with the women who came to the house for weekly bridge games and iced tea. G-Ma herself only got through those afternoons because her tea had a bit more than sugar added to it. Uncle Jack took Drew hiking and camping three or four times a year, but a boy needed more. G-Ma knew this. The school had been a good idea. Drew liked it on campus. His life was good at Winston School. At least it had been until the day Paige disappeared.

Drew walked along one of the outside paths that snaked around the three-hundred-acre campus. He'd been moving around in a daze since Paige went missing. Everything about the grounds looked the same, but it felt completely different. Winston had become a lot less idyllic than it used to be. He'd never questioned his safety at school before, and he doubted Paige had given it much thought, either.

Drew looked up to see a group of boys, most of them in the upper grades, engaged in a spirited game of basketball. His pace slowed as he walked past. He knew several of the players. One of them gave him a lazy wave and Drew studied Henry Wills, or Hank as he liked to be called.

Hank was a sophomore and three years older than Drew. They'd met last year when they wound up in the same art class. Drew still wasn't sure what had made him think that taking art was a good idea. Stick figures were a stretch for him, but Hank? Now that was a kid with real talent.

Drew sent a tentative wave back toward the court. He and Hank knew each other, but they'd never really been friends. They hung out with different groups, and Hank was an upper classman. He'd heard some stories about Hank, but the two of them had always co-existed just fine.

Mrs. Dunleavy, one of the biology teachers, was sitting on a bench outside Mitchell Hall. Drew didn't think she was part of the faculty that lived on campus, so he was surprised to see her on the grounds on a Saturday afternoon. She called to someone, and Drew moved his eyes to see a small girl running across the lawn. She had blonde pigtails and held a large butterfly net in one tight fist.

"There's one!" Mrs. Dunleavy leaned forward and pointed into the air. The grassy area was surrounded by dogwood trees, the largest of them standing twenty-five feet tall against the brilliant blue sky. The little girl swung her net trying to catch some of the red leaves that had fallen from the branches above her. Swipe, swipe, swipe.

The child brought the net close to her face and grinned. "Look, Mommy! I caught three of them! Three butterflies. Aren't they pretty?"

Drew watched her for a moment. The leaves did sort of resemble butterflies, he thought. A Lacewing, perhaps, or maybe an Atlas Moth. The little girl had an imagination. He liked that in a person. He smiled—something he hadn't done in a while—and made his way to his dorm.

His shoes thudded on the stairs as he climbed to the second floor. He could hear music coming from an open door down the hall and knew his roommate, Brice, was inside. Brice was a new kid. He seemed nice enough, but he'd brought a lot of stuff with him when he'd come to Winston.

Drew didn't know him very well, but he was fairly certain that Brice and G-Ma wouldn't make fast friends. One of her favorite sayings was "A place for everything and everything in its place". Drew wasn't all that surprised when he stepped inside and saw clothes draped over every available surface. He was glad G-Ma wasn't anywhere near his dorm room.

"Really, dude?" he asked, the momentary lift in his mood taking another downward turn. Drew walked over to his desk, his eyebrows drawn together as he noticed a pair of Captain America boxers flung over the back of his chair.

"All the dryers were being used," Brice said in way of explanation. He was lying on his bed tossing a baseball up into the air. He caught it—*thunk!*— then threw it again. "I have some rope somewhere. I thought about using it as a clothesline."

"That would have saved me from having to do my history homework with wet underwear at my back."

"Eh," Brice shrugged him off. "That sounds like a lot of work. Besides, they're almost dry."

Drew sighed. This school year was off to an awful start.

"Hey," Brice said as Drew unzipped his backpack. "What's up with that Henry Wills kid?"

He dropped the history book on his desk and turned to give Brice a squinty-eyed look. Drew rarely gave Hank a second thought, but here he was being brought to Drew's attention again. "Met him already, have you?" He dug around and gathered two pencils and a pen.

"I got called to the office this morning. It was something about the pants I wore yesterday. I call them khaki, but the Head Master calls them gray." He shrugged. "What do I know? I've been color blind since forever." *Thunk.* The baseball landed in the well-oiled palm of Brice's glove. "Anyway, he ran into me as he was walking out. Hit me so hard I almost fell over. Pissed me off 'cause he had plenty of room."

"It was probably an accident."

Brice didn't look convinced. "Whatever. I doubt me and Henry will ever travel in the same social circles."

"Probably not if you call him Henry."

Brice looked confused. He stopped throwing the baseball. "Why wouldn't I?"

"He doesn't like it. Matty Griner wound up with a black eye last year." He slapped a spiral notebook next to the history text and tossed the backpack on his bed. "There was some debate at the time about why Matty got smacked. A bunch of kids said it was because Matty used Hank's given name. Some others thought Hank was in a bad mood because Tabitha Haney had just dumped him." He shrugged. "I don't know. To be honest, I don't care. The lesson I took from the whole thing was that it's probably safer to call him Hank."

Drew plopped down in his chair, mindful not to lean back against the damp Captain. Brice threw his ball toward the ceiling again. *Thunk!* Drew shook his head. He didn't see his struggling grades improving anytime soon.

"So," Brice said, changing the subject. "Did you know the girl that disappeared? What's her name? Pamela? Peggy?"

"Paige." Drew spun around in his seat. His voice was harsher than he'd meant it to be, but he wasn't sorry for it. "Her name is Paige Carson, and yes, I know her."

Brice sat up and swung his feet to the floor. "Sorry, man. I didn't realize y'all were friends."

"Whatever." Drew turned around again, feeling tears sting the backs of his eyes.

"What do you think happened to her?"

Drew bit the inside of his cheek. He'd talked to Paige less than an hour before the police suspected she'd gone missing. She'd shown him the two new charms she'd gotten for her bracelet over the summer. One second, she was gushing about her new jewelry and the next she was telling him about how excited she was that she and a bunch of her friends had managed to gather enough girls to start an unofficial flag football league. They were set to have their first practice that afternoon. He loved that about Paige. She was feminine and girly but bad ass and tough all at the same time.

"I don't know," Drew answered, his eyes closed and his back still to Brice. It was true. Nothing about Paige's disappearance made sense to him. The only thing he knew for certain was that she hadn't gone anywhere on her own. If she'd left the campus, it was because someone had taken her.

...

Drew came out of sleep slowly, not knowing what it was that had pulled him from his dreams. He kept his eyes closed and listened. What was that sound?

He rolled over, trying to ignore it. It was faint and oddly familiar. He gave up and tried to blink away the darkness, but it was so black it felt as though he wore a blindfold over his eyes.

"Brice?"

Drew could hear the other boy snoring softly from his side of the room. The noise was obviously not bothering him.

What was that? Drew knew he wouldn't be able to get back to sleep again and climbed out of bed. He'd get in trouble if he was found roaming the grounds in the middle of the night, but now that he was awake he felt restless. He stuffed his feet into a pair of sneakers and quietly left the room.

Patches of clouds moved across the sky, the moon playing hide and seek behind them. It was chilly, somewhat breezy, and Drew could smell the change of the seasons as the air softly moved his over long bangs across his forehead. There it was again. Drew squinted as if that would make it easier to listen. That was the sound of a shovel. Someone was digging.

Drew followed the noise, mindful of alerting any of the faculty to his illegal nighttime activities. The sound grew louder as he walked through the main courtyard and around the science building. In another few minutes, he spotted a figure moving beneath a copse of trees. Drew squinted again, this time trying to separate the movements of human and shadow.

Was that Hank? What was it with this guy, anyway?

It only took a second for Drew to realize that it was Hank, and that he was standing beside a large hole. The blade of the shovel glinted momentarily in the silvery moonlight. There was something else resting by the jagged edge of torn grass. Something long. Something covered by a light covered fabric. A sheet? Drew wasn't sure.

He watched as Hank tried to move the covered object. When the older boy gave it a hearty nudge with his booted foot it rolled, and part of the sheet fell to the ground revealing something pale. Drew's stomach clenched when he realized what it was.

It was an arm. Around the wrist shone a hint of gold. A charm bracelet. Paige's charm bracelet.

"Oh, my God..." Drew breathed, immediately reaching up to cover his mouth with the palm of his hand. The world closed in around him, and he thought he might pass out. No. This couldn't be happening. This had to be a nightmare. He was still upstairs in the dark, nestled in the warmth of his bed listening to Brice snore in his sleep. This was unreal. This was Stephen King crap, and Drew really hated horror fiction.

He turned and ran around the corner of the building, hitting full speed as he reached the courtyard. The soles of his shoes slipped on the grass, and his arms flailed wildly in an attempt to keep him upright as he thundered up the steps of Clay Hall.

"No," he whispered to himself as bile built up in the back of his throat. "No, no, no..."

He slipped into his room, the latch engaging as he fell against the door. He slid down, landing hard on his butt. He cried then, his sobs quiet at first then growing louder. Time passed. Thirty minutes? An hour? He wasn't sure, but eventually he woke Brice who sat up in his bed.

"What the hell, man? What's goin' on?" He reached over and turned on his bedside lamp. "Dude, are you crying again?"

Drew heard another noise, this time right outside the door. The breath caught in his throat and he stilled, his heart beating hard inside the cage of his chest. He felt something move against his hand, and he jerked it quickly away. When he looked down he saw a sheet of paper as it was pushed beneath the door.

"Drew?" Brice asked.

"Shhh!" Drew shushed him. He screwed his eyes shut and listened as footsteps sounded in the hall once more, this time retreating. He swallowed, then opened his eyes very slowly. If there had been a doubt in his mind that it had been Hank he'd seen outside, what he was looking at now wiped it completely away.

It was a drawing done in pencil. He didn't know many people who could render the human face with such precision and expertise as this. No, the person who had drawn this had taken his time, studied his subject long and hard and had come up with a perfect replica of the real thing. It was Paige staring back at him from the rough, white sketch paper. Her eyes were wide and full of fear. Her lips were slightly parted, and she looked utterly terrified.

Drew realized that he and Henry Mills would never peacefully co-exist again.

"Hank," Drew whispered, his fingertips running across the black lines that had been drawn so carefully. "Paige is dead, and Hank killed her."

Brice's eyes fluttered in surprise before he fell back against his pillows again. He threw his arm over his face and sighed. "Unbelievable," he sighed. "If I'd wanted to live with these kinds of freak show antics, I would've just stayed at home."

In the Pursuit of Spring
A Very Dramatic Story About the Month of March

The young woman's arm, outstretched and hanging over the shiny red metal of the car in which she rode, bucked gently in the wind. Her fingers were flat, held together loosely in a lazy mock salute, and her hand rode the air currents that rushed past the open window. Clouds were forming in the sky looking like swollen dirty cotton balls as they rolled in and began spitting a thin cold rain that dotted the pale protruding limb. The only color she could see was the bright neon pink polish she'd picked up on sale a few days ago at the mall that covered her short oval nails like enthusiastic little flags moving in the chilly wind. March comes in like a lion so the old saying goes, and that was the truth of it. What used to be the beginning of a ten-month year many, many years ago in ancient Rome was arriving quickly on the coat tails of winter, full of boisterous bluster much like the growling and grumbling in the back of a big African cat's throat. The winter days following the Roman Decembris and those leading up to Martius, or this time of heralding spring, were so dreary and forgettable that at one time they were not even counted or assigned to any specific month. The girl quirked her mouth and watched the expanse of the cold and colorless sky hovering high above her dotted window and did not even think to wonder why this had been the case.

Round brown eyes squinted against the oncoming rain, while the clouds above her began to fold and shift as if they'd heard her silent unkind thoughts and were unnerved by them. Slowly, they transformed and began to resemble thick plumes of smoke rising from the ruins of a city demolished in heated dusty battle.

From within the amorphous swirls of darkening silver and gray the girl almost believed she could see the figure of a man, tall and broad shouldered carrying a spear in one meaty fist, the weapon wrapped in a thick vine of long-leafed laurel. Mars, the god of war and ultimate pastoral guardian, looked to be treading upon an unstable ground of moving soot with a pair of large feet clad in roughly laced, flat soled sandals. His hairy unclothed legs beneath a short and flared skirt looked strong and undeniably masculine as he motioned time itself to move forward with a wave of his powerful arm. The thirty-one days of this unpredictable month boasted the name of this esteemed mythological deity who was said to have used his military power to secure peace, and each minute ticked by like an attentive and patient soldier in his army as the water continued to fall from the sky and slowly erased from view the swirling clouds that moved above the speeding car. With a turn of a head accompanied by a pair of raised eyebrows from the front passenger seat, the girl grudgingly acquiesced to the wordless maternal request, first tossing a temperamental roll of her eyes before moving her wet arm into the warmth of the vehicle as the window whirred silently upward and locked itself back into the frame. Almost instantly the glass was covered in a countless array of dots of cool rain, each one a round wet orb that splintered and multiplied her view of the outside world. If there had been a question of the god of war's existence just moments before it was all but obliterated now as the sleek lines of the car moved quickly above wet pavement, throwing up a pair of plumes the color of rotting and filthy ice behind the rear tires. The clouds above continued to roll and churn as the chill in the interior of the car was chased away by the warm stale air spewing from the vents in the dash board. The change in temperature and the weather outside stubbornly limited her view with a mist of milky fog on one side of the glass and a kaleidoscope of raindrops on the other. With a hushed and defeated sigh, the teen relaxed in her seat, her carefully coiffed blonde head pressed against the soft pliable leather as the film of limitless road and soft-edged scenery slid past in a watery and colorless blur.

While she listened to the rhythmic beat of windshield wipers as they cleared the driver's view in the front seat, the story of the conspiracy and brutal assassination of Julius Caesar, believed by many to be one of the greatest military commanders in history, marched quietly and unbidden into her head. Just like the wipers soothed her now, so had the tale, or perhaps more the telling of the tale in the flowing and somewhat lyrical style of Shakespeare's iambic pentameter, the words rolling and almost musical coming from the throat of her teacher as she'd read it aloud in school months before. English, not one of her favorite subjects if she was honest, was situated tortuously before the forty minutes of freedom that was lunch break and was normally a span of time she put up with only because she had no other choice in the matter. However, and she was at least mature enough to admit this, but only to those who were closest to her and who would not dare repeat it, she'd found the steady, confident lift and fall of the aforementioned teacher's voice surprisingly pleasant as she'd recited the dying words of the infamous Roman general, uttered while the man is being brutally murdered by a group of ruthless men at the Senate. "Et tu, Brute? Then fall, Caesar," the dying man whispers as he pulls the white fabric of a toga over his face and dramatically falls dead and bleeding from numerous swipes and stabs of malicious blades upon the ground on that ill-fated day now remembered as the Ides of March.

The girl was relatively certain that it mattered little if nothing at all to her whether or not Caesar had actually been militarily brilliant, and it had been consistently pointed out to her by her teacher that Shakespeare's telling of the story was a bit historically askew, so it was the fictitious facts of that long ago day she'd been interested in, if only long enough to pass the quarter final. She was pretty sure that she'd gotten the most important parts of the story down, although some of the details had been less than clear with too many characters to keep track of, and all of them speaking a language that was far too frilly and nearly undecipherable to her teen ears.

During the course of the nine weeks her class had studied the literary piece she oftentimes found herself thinking that Shakespeare was highly over rated and had decided halfway through the first act of the play that a writer as praised as the famous old Brit was should be a little easier to understand. As the girl slowly drifted to that hazy place that lingers just before sleep, a thoughtful and perhaps mischievous smile played along the line of her carefully painted lips. A soothsayer's warning and an adoring wife's bloody premonition be damned. Sometimes, and the occasion was rare she was certain, it just didn't pay to be stubborn.

Behind her now closed eyes a vision began to take shape, one of many a teen girl's dreams in the shape of a handsome hulking vampire with a very unsexy moniker that hardly matched the body seen beneath the Calvin Klein underwear he was known to model in the glossy and perfumed pages of countless fashion magazines. The fifteenth day of March had not been so lucky for old Caesar, the girl thought, but that was way back in 44 BC. It was so hard to mourn the death of someone she never even knew when more than 2,000 years later, God saw fit to bring a being like Kellan Lutz into the world on that very same day. "Friends, Romans, countrymen, lend me your ears," she mused as her smile widened just for a moment with the thought that the Ides of March was not entirely unlucky before she allowed the thump of the wipers and the movement of the car to lull her even closer into the land of dreams. "Kellan Lutz is born!" the anonymous announcer in her head continued to shout enthusiastically. "And pre-adolescent girls worldwide rejoice!"

It felt as though winter had shown up, liked the surroundings and settled itself for an interminable amount of time with its sharp claws imbedded firmly into the very fabric of the young woman's being.

The grayness and bitter temperatures seemed more like a pair of permanent residents instead of short term seasonal visitors, and the twitch beneath her skin that felt a lot like spring time had grown into an uncontrollable itch that no amount of scratching could diminish.

This girl was definitely no snow bunny, and the bleak white canvas filled with nothing but shadows of screeching dark winged birds and tall scraggly arms of bare trees reaching eerily up into the dense milky sky had her inner beach bum screaming to be heard. The girl longed for March's lions, their honey colored coats warm and soft, their eyes dark green with spots of red the color of bloodstones, to stalk across the sky on big padded paws and pull from behind their muscled backs the wide warm banners of crisp aquamarine like bright Mardi Gras flags brightening up the bleak sky to usher in the first day of spring. Nothing could bring out the drama queen in this sun worshipping female more than winter's colorless and never ending cold and snow, and no doubt the Old Bard himself would have happily awarded her over enthusiastic mental ramblings a well-deserved round of applause.

She barely heard the noise at first, so immersed in her silent and subconscious diatribe against the cheerlessness of the first two months of the year that it took her mind a handful of minutes to register the incessant tapping somewhere near the vicinity of her right elbow. She slit one brown eye partially open and slowly focused on the culprit; one small but chubby and rather dirty looking troll strapped tightly into a heavy-duty car seat which rested snugly beside her.

There were small square shaped books with hard unbendable pages and a cup with a supposedly spill proof lid leaking a suspicious honey colored liquid that smelled like sweet white grapes lying across a pair of rather round and denim-clad legs. On the ends of those legs were two kicking feet in stained white sneakers keeping time with the almost lyrical gibberish flowing out of the toddler's graham cracker encrusted mouth, the untied laces flapping and moving about like restless and uncoordinated snakes around his ankles.

The boy's hair was several shades darker than his older sisters with shiny curls that stuck out at wild angles around his face that gave him the look of a very young but energetic rock star. The girl wanted to be annoyed by the interruption of her nap, but upon resting her eyes on her baby brother's plump pink tinted cheeks, she found herself smiling at him instead. Okay, so he wasn't really a troll she silently conceded. A pixie, maybe, or perhaps a leprechaun. Yes, she decided with an unenergetic forward dip of her pointed chin, that's what he is. He's a leprechaun, though admittedly much cuter than most she'd seen depicted in books or movies, but still as short and unruly.

The stripes that trailed along the fabric of the young boy's long sleeved shirt were the bright green color of the three-leaved shamrocks that St. Patrick used to teach the Trinity to the pagan Irish, each one representing God as the Father, the Son and the Holy Spirit, and the gap-toothed grin that brightened the little imp's face as he twisted in his chair to look at his sister made the corners of her own mouth lift a bit higher. The only rainbow this little leprechaun was liable to lead her to was perhaps a pilfered package of colorful Skittles candy broken open and spilled on the pantry floor, or a bright array of building blocks that hurt the tender insteps of her feet when she tried to traverse the messy landscape of the child's room in the dark. As for a pot of gold, well, she quietly laughed. That was, without a doubt, completely out of the question.

She reached for the upended cup and felt the stickiness of the juice coat the pads of her fingers. Score another point for false advertising, she mused. The lid was definitely not spill proof, but who in the world would notice after looking at the mess her brother had become since he'd climbed into the car seat more than an hour before?

"Be like the Irish, little man," she said quietly as she handed the cup over to him. The little sprite reached over with a pudgy hand and gladly took it from her. "Drink up." When he wrapped his lips around the spout and took a pull from it the girl laughed again. With that diaper of his bowing his short little legs, he walked a bit like a drunkard much like any other toddler she'd ever seen, and without a nap, he was nearly as surly and cantankerous as a few of the drunks she'd encountered. Yes, a leprechaun made the most sense. She wondered why she'd never come to the realization before.

With a shake of her head she turned and peered out of her window once more to find that the thick veil of clouds had finally begun to part. The rain was still spitting at her window but with much less intensity, and the drone of the windshield wipers had slowed to a sluggish beat. She had to squint to see it, but she was sure that the tiny little triangle of sky she spied behind the gray curtain was actually a faint shade of blue. Her eyes held fast to it as if they were daring it to change while she remained ever hopeful that it wouldn't. Indeed, it was the pale soft color of a robin's egg nestled in a nest, and the shell grew a little bit bigger as she focused on it, the cars and highway signs a blur in her peripheral vision.

Gradually, the rain let up altogether, and what it left behind was a world now shiny and clean if not still a bit chilled by the cool air. It looked reborn, almost fragile in its new state, and as the clouds let go their grip on the threads of their fabric, and the weave became increasingly loose, more of the watery blue sky was revealed. The girl silently coaxed the sun out of its den like she would a baby bird out of its shell. "Come on out," she silently urged, the voice in her head gentle and soothing. "Come out and meet this cold winter world that needs your heat and light." As if it had actually been listening to her, the soft gleam of sun peeked through, it's rays as warm and soft as thick creamy butter burned off more of the clouds, and ever so faintly there appeared to be the smallest hint of a rainbow, the streams barely creating the merest suggestion of pastel pink, yellow, blue and green reflected in the moisture that still clung wetly to the cool air.

The car slowed and veered right off the highway, and the quiet clicking sound of the blinker faintly filled the warm air inside the vehicle. Smoothly, the girl's father turned left, and the scenery from the other side of the window moved but not on high speed as before. The girl caught glimpses of shiny rain-washed windows glinting in the increasingly courageous rays of the sun above, and the bare limbs of the trees were showing small tightly folded buds dotted along their wooden sleeves like little decorative buttons. Dirt as dark as coal filled planters and roadside gardens, the brave thick stalks buried beneath pushing through with the bright color of emeralds and sporting long wrapped hats the shade of downy feathers on a newly hatched chick.

A smile floated across the teen's glossy lips once more as she peered up and watched the movement of the clouds, their shape rounded and snowy white now and moving across the sky like a herd of lazily grazing sheep, their coats fluffy clean and white. As she watched them she was convinced that these were March's lambs slowly and hesitantly following the thunderous noise of the rambunctious, lean-bodied lions, and she decided that she liked them just fine. Yes, she thought with a self-satisfied smile as the reflection of the fat white flock moved against the wide brown of her upturned and unblinking eyes. She liked them very much indeed.

Some Things Just Are
A Personal Essay
August 10, 2016

My dad has been gone now for more than fifteen years. I wasn't there when he died. We were estranged for seven years before the first heart attack put him in the hospital and the second one killed him, but I'm not sure any of that matters when it comes to being family. He's my dad. He'll always be my dad. There are some things that just are.

I haven't looked into my dad's face for more than twenty years ... but I see him each and every time I look in the mirror. His eyes were hazel—more of a dark brown—and mine are blue/green, but the shape is the same; enormous and round. I got my long eyelashes from him as well. He used to tell me they were so long that I had dinosaurs living on them. See? That's what I do. I cling to every single good thing, no matter how small. That's me ... a true optimist at heart. He told me more times than I could count how unattractive I was while I was growing up ... but in reality, I look a lot like him.

My dad was an addict. He was addicted to alcohol, and he was addicted to drugs. He could fully commit to those things. Family life? Not so much. After he passed away, my mom sent me an article that had been written (by a friend, no doubt) who wrote for the Denver Post. This journalist listed off a whole lot of great attributes he claimed my father had. I was tempted to call this guy up and have a little chat with him, let him know that he'd probably make millions as a fantasy writer.

My father was twenty-three when I was born. He and my mom had an on again, off again kind of relationship, and it surprised me later when I heard he'd shown up at all after my birth. I was named Jennifer because he didn't like the name my mother had chosen. I've always resented my name. One reason was that every other little girl born around the same time was given the name—but mostly because my dad chose it for me.

My parents tied the knot when I was eighteen months old, and then were divorced, after an incredibly rocky marriage, when I was five. For the next eleven years, I watched him struggle with addiction, all the while thinking that it was the drugs and alcohol that made him the destructive, angry, mean, loud person that he was. My dad didn't talk. You didn't have a conversation with him—or at least I didn't. He yelled. I looked down at my hands and tried not to cry—crying made him angry—and he yelled. He could throw an insult like no other and cut me to the quick without even trying.

When I was twelve or thirteen, my mom pulled me out of school for a week during the winter so that I could go up to Estes Park and take part in a family counseling session at a recovery program my dad was in. It was a rough week. I did a lot of bonding—but not with my dad. I had a lot in common with the other family members in attendance, but, even though it was in a controlled environment, I was terrified. I couldn't tell him what I thought or felt about our relationship. He was calmer there, further encouraging the mindset that the substances he abused were the cause of his demonstrative personality. But the program didn't stick. He was drinking and using again not long after he came home. It wasn't the first time the idea of abstinence refused to take hold ... and it wouldn't be the last.

There were times I couldn't take it anymore; times when the physical and emotional abuse got to be too much, and I'd separate myself from him. I remember being at a friend's house one afternoon. She lived a couple doors down from me, and I saw my dad's red van drive down the street. I panicked and ran and hid on her stairs. He'd come to make up with me. There were never any apologies. He'd laugh and joke and tease me about not being able to handle my "mean old man". His words. It was always me who couldn't handle things. He was never at fault. I was always too sensitive. It was one of the many negative qualities he found in my personality. I didn't go to my house that afternoon while he was there, but eventually I went to seek him out. He was my dad. I was a child. I always felt like he deserved another chance ... and I gave him many, many chances.

After several attempts, he finally got sober when I was sixteen. Over the next five years, I realized that it wasn't the alcohol or the drugs that made my dad the way he was. Slowly, (and reluctantly) I came to the conclusion that my dad was just an asshole. That's a hard thing to resolve in your head and in your heart at any age, but I know that with all certainty now.

The day I found out that my father had passed away, I was a mess of emotions. My family, kind as they are, wanted to be there for me, but they had no idea what to do. My aunt Deene sent me a card. She stated that however I was feeling was the right way for me to feel. It sounds simplistic, but seeing those words written out that way made all my mixed-up emotions suddenly seem okay for me.

I was sad ... I'd given up. There had never been a resolution to our incredibly screwed up relationship in large part because I couldn't take the abuse any longer. Maybe if I'd worked harder, things would have been resolved.

Then there was anger. I hate to admit this, but I was angry that he'd had the nerve to die. I was punishing him. I had pushed him out of my life because he didn't deserve me, and he bailed on that punishment by dying. Screwed up? Yes. Wrong? I don't know. I guess the truth is, I don't care how others see it, or how others feel about it. Like I stated before—some things just are. They can't be changed.

I loved my dad. If I hadn't, none of what we went through would have meant anything or been as difficult as it was. I loved him ... but I've never liked him very much. I don't suppose I ever will.

A Day in Paris
A Countdown Story

Justine quickly walked up the wide stairway in front of the Gare de Marseille-Saint-Charles. It was an old train station, built on top of a hill in 1848. She counted the steps aloud as she ascended, her voice growing breathier as she finally reached the last of seven landings. One hundred and four. Just as she'd remembered from her childhood.

She turned and looked down at the city of Marseille below her. She had many good memories of growing up here, and she'd enjoyed her stay, but it was time to go back home now. Time to get back to Theo.

Justine clutched the ticket in her hand. There was a line at the check-in counter nearly ten people long. She brushed her sun streaked hair out of her face and took her place behind an older gentleman wearing a gray suit and tie.

"Bonjour," he greeted, the light from above glinting in the small, round surfaces of his eye glasses.

"Bonjour, monsieur," Justine replied with a smile. "Comment allez-vous?"

"Bien, merçi. Et vous?"

"Ah," Justine said with a dip of her chin. "Bien, aussi. Trés bien."

And she was very well indeed. She was on her way home to Paris to see her son after playing nursemaid for nearly a month. Juliette was great, as far as sisters went, but no one was better company than her Theo. Oh, how she missed that child.

The line moved forward, and soon she was pulling her suitcase behind her toward the train that would take her past Avignon and over the Loire River as it made its way toward Lyon and then Paris. The little wheels spun and jumped as they worked to keep up with her. She glanced quickly at the signs and politely dodged other passengers as she hurried to the designated track.

She beat the train by a quarter of an hour, and by the time it pulled up and the doors opened, she'd memorized the information printed on her ticket. She picked up her suitcase and draped her jacket over her arm before stepping inside.

It was easy enough to find the right car, and once she was there, she tipped her blue eyes upward and scanned the numbers above each row of seats. That's it, she thought to herself as she arrived at the correct location. A young, dark-haired girl sat near the window. She looked up as Justine dropped lightly into seat number nine. The girl offered her a shy smile and Justine returned it.

"Hello," the child said, her words dripping with a deep British accent. "I'm Alice. I'm on holiday."

"Very well then, Alice," Justine responded in well-practiced English. "It's a pleasure to meet you." She held her hand out and Alice gave it a shake. "You're rather young to be traveling alone cross country, aren't you?"

"I'm eight," the girl informed her. "But small for my age."

"Hmmm, I see," Justine said with an understanding nod.

"And I'm not traveling alone," she admitted. "Mum and Dad are a few rows back. The train was nearly full, and I got to sit by myself."

Justine looked around, surveying the car. "It is full, isn't it?" She looked back at Alice. "Everyone is eager to visit Paris. June is the perfect time of year for it, you know?"

"I've never been."

Justine smiled. "I think you're going to love it."

"Do you visit much?"

"Actually, I live in Paris."

"On a beach holiday, then?"

"Not exactly," Justine explained. "You see, my sister, my very, very clumsy sister, Juliette, had an accident. I've been in Marseille helping her rehabilitate."

"Oh, no!" Alice exclaimed. "Was she hurt badly?"

"Yes. It was her leg. Broken, I'm afraid, with a cast up to here." She tapped the middle of her thigh. "But now that she has done a bit of healing, I'm going back home. My son, Theo, is waiting for me."

"Have you missed him?"

"You have no idea," Justine sighed dramatically. The child laughed. "He's exactly your age. He's not small, though. In another few years, I fear he'll be as tall as I am."

The train had begun moving while the two had been having their chat, and Alice turned her head to watch the scenery. "How long will it take to get to Paris?"

"A few hours. Did you bring something to pass the time?"

Alice nodded. "A book."

"Brilliant," Justine said, digging into her purse. "How would your parents feel about me sharing some sweets?"

Alice watched as her seat mate pulled out a cellophane bag full of peppermint candies. "Oh," she said. "They wouldn't mind a bit."

Justine smiled and poured seven of the treats into Alice's cupped hands. "Suck on them, don't chew. That way you save your teeth and make them last throughout the trip."

Alice unwrapped one of the candies and popped it into her mouth. "Thank you," she said as she opened her book and began to read.

...

In Paris, there are six large main-line railway terminals. Paris-Gare de Lyon was one of them, situated on the north bank of the river Seine in the eastern part of the city.

As soon as the train had pulled into the station, Justine waited until Alice was reunited with her parents before bidding her adieu. After she freed herself from the knot of people on the platform, she found herself tempted by a menu posted outside Le Train Bleu.

The entrance to the restaurant was ornate; golden gilding and carvings, beautiful arches adorned with angels, wings aflutter. Opened to celebrate the Great Exhibition of 1900, the dining establishment had served a list of esteemed guests. The list included Jean Cocteau, Coco Chanel, and Brigitte Bardot. Justine had eaten at Le Train Bleu a few times, although not with any celebrities. She had read Agatha Christie's bestselling novel, *The Mystery of the Blue Train*, though. She'd enjoyed both the restaurant and the novel tremendously.

Her stomach grumbled, and she pulled out her phone, touching the screen to bring it to life. It was nearly noon. No wonder she was hungry. For just a minute, she longed to sit on one of the ornate seats upholstered in royal blue fabric and eat a leg of lamb with potatoes cooked with Fourme d'Ambert cheese. Another quiet groan from beneath her belt brought her out of her reverie. She shook her head, and the thought of gourmet cuisine, out of her mind. She had Theo to get to. She'd pick something up to snack on while she made her way to their meeting place.

Justine stepped out into the sunshine and took a breath of summer time air. The sky was a brilliant blue and she squinted, reaching into her purse for a pair of sunglasses. She hailed one of the taxi's waiting for a fare and pulled her suitcase into the car beside her.

"Notre Dame," she told the driver after a moment's thought. She turned her head to catch a glimpse of the ornate clock tower that faced Boulevard Diderot, the street on which they were traveling. She'd seen it many times, and, as always, it reminded her of Big Ben. She smiled when Alice came to mind and wondered if the child might also see the resemblance.

The traffic was heavy as it always was, and Justine tried to relax as the driver deftly maneuvered the vehicle. She'd been sitting for too long and looked forward to the walk she had ahead of her. Theo would be meeting her on the other side of the city. She could easily take the taxi all the way to Quai Branly where he would be waiting, but he wouldn't be there for another couple of hours. She'd missed her city and knew by taking a leisurely stroll, she'd be giving Paris the opportunity to welcome her back home.

"Ici, s'il vous plait," she said, leaning forward in her seat. She saw the driver's eyes move upward in the rearview mirror.

"D'accord," he responded, pulling the car over on Quai de la Tournelle. She handed him twenty euros, and as he made change, she looked up to see that they were near the Pont de l'Archeveche, or Archbishop's Bridge. It was a road bridge, but quite narrow. As she walked toward it, pulling her suitcase along she thought she remembered Theo telling her that it was the narrowest road bridge in all of Paris.

Years earlier, when the Pont d'Arts was relieved of all the love locks that had been placed there, everyone decided to start attaching their padlocks on this bridge instead. There were so many of them, all in different colors and glinting warmly in the sun. As Justine walked above the stone arches, she reached her hand out, and her fingers skipped along five of the locks. They were warm to the touch and clicked together when she touched them. She and Theo's father had taken part in this Parisian tradition years before their son had been born. He had engraved their initials upon the metal of their chosen lock before going out and attaching the token of love among the hundreds of others.

But that had been years ago, back when they had been young. Back when Mathis had still been alive. Justine hadn't retrieved it before they'd cut the heavy assortment of love locks from Pont d'Arts. She imagined that the one that had belonged to them was at the bottom of the Seine, buried among the debris that resided there.

Justine sighed, her head turned to the left. Notre Dame rose high into the sky and she blinked away tears. She veered left onto Rue du Cloître Notre Dame and came upon the cathedral and all the tourists who swarmed around it. Happy, smiling people on holiday, in awe of the sights that inhabited her beautiful city.

She smiled and tipped her head, seeing four pigeons perched nonchalantly atop Stryga's head. The sight made her laugh, and she pushed her sunglasses higher on the bridge of her nose. It was hard to see him well from where she stood, but she thought he looked a bit angry with the birds, his chin resting in the palms of both hands, his beastly mouth formed into a rounded pout. He was supposed to be scary, but the pigeons were largely unaffected by his monstrous appearance. Aside from the hunchback himself, Stryga was perhaps the most famous resident of Notre Dame, often called the spitting gargoyle. Justine knew better. He was a chimera. Theo had told her so.

She turned left again in front of the cathedral onto Place Jean Paul II where she crossed the Seine once more, this time walking over Pont au Double. Her stomach protested again, annoyed that it had been ignored for so long.

Justine followed the bank of the river and saw the pyramid in Cour Napoléon wink at her. The sun was reflecting off the glass and metal, advertising the location of the Louvre better than any marquee. It was time to appease the hungry gremlin in her belly, and this was the perfect place to do so. She chose a spot in her favorite outdoor café and plopped herself down as she watched the museum goers move toward the Palais du Louvre.

If there was a better place to people watch than Paris, Justine couldn't fathom where it might be. She sipped on her café crème, one of three she decided to order, while nibbling the pain au chocolat that rested on a plate in the center of her small table. The crust was flaky and tasted of butter, but the real treat was the bittersweet chocolate, all warm and gooey, that was tucked inside. She took her time with the pastry, feeling the heat of the sun as it shone on her face.

She watched as tourists passed by the café, their hands busy with métro maps, and their necks adorned with expensive cameras. There was so much to see, and she smiled inwardly at the unconcealed masks of fascination they all seemed to wear on their faces.

Her hunger abated, Justine pulled herself from her comfortable seat and continued her trek. La Tour Eiffel loomed in the distance, and she felt a tingle of anticipation stir within her. It had been a long month without Theo. Although they'd spoken on the phone every day, and they'd seen one another on their computer screens, she found that spending time with him from a distance was a poor substitute for the real thing. She loved her sister but had decided within days of arriving in Marseille that Juliette needed to learn to be more careful.

"Maman!" She started at the sound of his voice and looked up to see her son running toward her.

"Theo!" she yelled back, her heart swelling at the sight of him. "Je suis donc heureux de vous voir!" From over his bobbing blond head Justine spotted Sophie, her dear friend who had moved into the flat she and Theo shared while Justine had been away.

The boy ran to his mother, nearly knocking her over in his excitement. She laughed and mussed his hair with her fingers before bending to take his head between both of her hands. His eyes were wide and round, and she gave him two sound kisses, first on his right cheek and then on his left.

"Salut," she told him, still smiling.

"Je vous ai manqué," he responded. Justine nodded in agreement. She'd missed him, too.

She opened her arms. "Embrasse-moi serré et ne jamais laisser aller," she told him. He gave her a dazzling smile and did as she'd asked, wrapping his arms tightly around her in one gigantic hug.

Remembrance

Raindrops or moonbeams,
never matters anyway
Time to go—see you again,
Maybe
As I watch you leave,
wave and I'll see it
Remember it was real once
and I'll stop and feel you there.

1/88

Return to Blue River

Darius had been traveling for months on end. That's what had attracted him to the job in the first place, what had lured him away from the quiet, small town he felt he'd outgrown. He'd been fascinated by the idea of seeing places he'd never visited before and doing it on his new employer's dime seemed like a brilliant way to do it.

The first few trips hadn't gone smoothly. Being in the middle of the chaos and the bustle of seasoned travelers had been intimidating in the beginning. It had also been exhilarating. He didn't worry too much when, during the first half dozen trips, he saw nothing more than a glimpse of each new city while in a cab going from the airport and back again. Everything required a bit of practice, he surmised. As soon as he'd figured out the logistics of getting to and from each new place, he was sure he'd find some time that wasn't taken up by work responsibilities in which to enjoy his destination.

That had been good in theory. Reality turned out to be altogether different.

Packing, transportation, security and boarding were all things that Darius mastered. No matter how skilled he became with the process, however, he still couldn't find a way to eke out any time for personal exploration.

His time was scheduled by an efficient secretary who made sure that Darius was in each of his destinations only long enough to check into a hotel, eat a questionable meal and attend whatever meeting he'd flown in for before making his way back to the airport again. She was paid to keep Darius on a strict budget, both with his time and the company's money, and she was good at her job. A little too good in his opinion.

He had nothing to prove that he'd been in nearly forty different cities in the past year except for a shelf full of overpriced paperback novels and a collection of refrigerator magnets that took up space in an apartment he rarely slept in.

He'd gone to St. Louis, but never saw the Gateway Arch. He'd had a meeting in Manhattan, but he and Lady Liberty never exchanged so much as a hello. He thought he might get a peek at the Space Needle, but he hadn't gotten a window seat on that flight. It didn't matter much anyway. His seat mate informed him that there was nothing to look at but fog.

The trip to D.C. had excited him, especially the thought of visiting the Lincoln Memorial, but the only thing he'd gotten to see was the Washington Monument, and that at a distance. The barbecue he'd tasted in North Carolina had not been nearly as amazing as he'd always heard it was, but then again, the pulled pork sandwich he'd ordered had been eaten in an airport restaurant and washed down with flat beer. As far as meals on the run went, though, it hadn't been the worst one he'd forced down.

Darius had become a nationwide traveler, but he hadn't gotten to see or experience a single damn thing.

The panel on the door switched from red to green, and Darius heard a tell-tale click that let him know the lock had been disengaged. He pushed the door open and walked into a room that resembled all the others he'd spent nights in over the past year. He put his bag down on the bed and reached up, rubbing his weary face with his palms.

How had it come to this? How had his life become this nomadic but unadventurous existence filled with wrinkled suit jackets steaming in hotel bathrooms and club sandwiches with cold fries delivered by room service?

Oh, yes, he sighed, sinking next to his bag on the mattress. He'd chosen it, right after he'd decided he was done living a small life in a small town. And right after he'd broken the heart of the one girl he loved the most in all the world.

...

More time passed. Darius navigated more airports, bought more magnets and ate more mediocre hotel meals. Spring turned to summer, and summer into fall. That tall pile of reasons he'd stacked up for leaving home seemed to shorten as the days, the weeks, and the months passed. He was starting to second guess many of the decisions he'd made in the past year.

When he got the first message from his little sister, Molly, telling him she was coming home in a few weeks for Thanksgiving, he smiled, thinking it would be great to see her again.

The second, third and fourth calls all came while he was either in meetings or taking off on another business trip and unable to answer his phone. He smiled a little less as he listened to Molly's voice in each of the messages.

"All of us would love to see you for the holiday."

"I'm dating someone. He's not coming with me to dinner, but I'd love to tell you about him."

"I miss you, big brother."

Molly talked about a great many things in her messages. The one thing she never mentioned was Madalyn.

...

Blue River, Colorado was only five miles south, and about a ten-minute drive, from downtown Breckenridge. That is if the weather was clear. The day Darius came back home it wasn't.

On average, about 130 inches of snow fell on the town of Blue River each year. That was a good thing since it was located so close to one of Colorado's most popular ski resorts. As Darius maneuvered his rented Explorer along state highway 9, he figured at least twenty-four of that 130 inches were already covering the ground.

He'd sent a brief text to Molly. He didn't want to ignore his sister, but he was intentionally vague in his response. If he didn't tell her he'd be there for Thanksgiving, he could still back out of it without breaking a promise to her. He'd already broken enough promises. He was done with that.

The house on Mountain View Drive had been built back in 1998. Before then, the Palmer family lived in Breckenridge proper where Will worked at the hospital and his wife, Jess, taught second grade. When the oldest Palmer child, Darius, was six, the family moved into the custom-built house that sat adjacent to the river. Four years after that, Molly was born. Darius hadn't seen his childhood home in nearly eighteen months. When he pulled the Explorer up and into the drive, he was surprised when he realized how much he'd missed it.

Darius listened to the engine ping as it cooled. The sky was filled with gray clouds that spit snowflakes out at him as he sat inside the truck. There were two other vehicles parked in the wide drive. He recognized Molly's red pickup. The other one, a white Blazer, didn't look at all familiar. He could tell there was writing on the door, but Darius couldn't read what it said from where he sat. There were only about 900 people living in Blue River. That had been one of the biggest issues for him before he left. He was almost sure he'd known, or at least met, all of them.

"Darius?"

He didn't hear her at first, but he saw her as she stepped out onto the covered porch. She wore a fleece lined coat, unzipped, and her copper colored hair was lifted by the frigid air that swirled more snow around her smiling face.

Darius grabbed his bag and slid from the truck. "Hey, Mol," he called to her with a wave of his hand. His booted feet crunched through the snow and caught her up in a tight embrace when she nearly jumped off the porch and into his arms.

"Mom and Dad didn't say a word about you being here," she said into the warm crook of his neck.

"That's because Mom and Dad didn't know I was coming."

Molly squeezed him even tighter. "Tell me you're staying for a while."

Darius moved his eyes around the front of the house. Time was a strange thing. More than a year had passed, but now that he was back, it felt as though he'd been here just yesterday. Everything about his family home looked the same. He remembered feeling trapped here, restless. The last time he'd been standing on this porch he'd wanted nothing more than to run away from it and never come back. He couldn't be sure, but what he felt now standing there with Molly seemed like something completely different.

"I don't know," he told his sister with a sigh. "We'll just have to wait and see."

...

He hadn't even gotten his coat off before Molly was announcing his arrival.

"Look who I found wandering around outside?"

"Not another bear I hope," Jess's voice filtered in from the kitchen.

"There have been bears?" Darius asked, his eyebrow cocked.

Molly brushed him off. "Not big ones."

"Oh," Jess said as she walked into the foyer, her mouth opened in surprise. "Darius!" Tears suddenly brightened her eyes. "I had no idea … I thought you were … well, my goodness … get yourself over here!" She laughed and hurried toward her son with her arms outstretched.

"Hey, Mom," he said, returning her enthusiastic hug.

From over his mother's shoulder he saw someone else come into the entry. Her head was down, and a phone was pressed to her ear. She was speaking but Darius couldn't hear what she was saying. The tone of her voice indicated something urgent was going on, and it looked like she was in a hurry. She grabbed a coat hanging near the entrance to Will's office and pushed her arms through the sleeves, holding the phone between her shoulder and her cheek as she zipped it up.

"I'll be there as soon as I can," she said before dropping the phone into her coat pocket and pulling a pair of thick mittens onto her hands. She stepped into a pair of boots, then looked up just as Jess was pulling away from her son. She caught Darius's glance and stopped moving for a moment, her eyes blinking rapidly.

"Hi, Maddie."

Madalyn regained her composure and quickly covered her blonde head with a cap that matched her mittens.

"Buttercup's in labor," she said walking past him. She opened the door and slipped out into the bitterly cold afternoon, the door settling back into the frame with a solid thunk. Darius watched her from one of the front windows, his eyes glued to the red bootlaces that trailed behind her in the snow as she hurried toward the blazer parked in front of the house.

"Buttercup?" he inquired.

"One of the Jamisons' cows," Jess filled in.

"Oh ..."

A few seconds later the door jiggled, then opened again. Darius expected to see Madalyn walk in. Instead it was a large man in a heavy parka who stepped inside the house.

Will looked at his son and his face split into a wide grin. "Well," he said stomping the snow from his boots onto the thick rug. "Glad to see you still know your way home, son." He pulled his coat off and hung it up before reaching down to untie his Sorels. "And I'm sure glad it's you on the property instead of that damn bear again."

...

Hours later, Darius sat in the kitchen with Molly. The day had been a pleasant one, filled with an amazing amount of food, football and conversation. It was nearly eleven now, and both Jess and Will had gone up to bed. The younger Palmers were raiding the fridge and sharing an almost midnight snack when they heard a knock on the back door.

"Got any mashed potatoes left?" Madalyn asked as Molly pulled the door open.

"Of course. Come on in. Damn, it's cold out there," Molly shivered as she threw the deadbolt back in place.

"Four degrees last time I checked. Snow's moving in again, too. We'll have another foot out there by morning I'll bet."

"I hope no more of Jamisons' cows are ready to deliver."

"Nope," Madalyn shook her head. "Buttercup was the only rebel in the herd. She saw a striking young bull and just couldn't help herself."

"Speaking of which ..." Molly turned, and Madalyn's gaze followed to where Darius sat at the island in the center of the kitchen, a knife in his hand and sandwich fixings scattered over the granite counter top.

"Sure took you a long time to deliver that calf," he said, licking a smear of mustard from his knuckle.

"Not quite as long as it took you to get your ass back home again," Madalyn volleyed back.

"Yeah," he agreed with a nod. "I guess it takes as long as it takes." They watched each other for a moment. "Everything come out okay?"

"For Buttercup it did. We'll have to wait to see how the rest of it plays out."

She unlaced her boots and kicked them off. Her hair was down and dotted with snowflakes. She was wearing a different sweater than she'd had on when she left, and her cheeks were pink with the cold.

"The Blazer belongs to you," Darius mused, layering thick slices of tomato on top of an already heaping sandwich.

"Summit County Veterinarian Clinic, actually, but yeah, I drive it more than anyone else does."

He cut the sandwich in half and slid the plate toward her. She hadn't moved from her place at the door yet, her eyes still on his face.

"Mustard, no mayo," he told her. "Just how you like it."

She looked at the open jar of mayonnaise sitting on the counter in front of him. "That one's yours," she replied. "I'll make my own."

"Come eat. You've been working all day."

"Not all day," she admitted walking slowly across the room. "The calf dropped pretty quickly."

"You've been gone for almost nine hours."

"I had some thinking to do." She climbed up onto the bar stool next to his and glanced up at Molly. The two girls held each other's gaze for a few seconds before Molly turned and retrieved some bowls covered with plastic wrap from the fridge. Madalyn looked back over at Darius. "You know all about that, right? Needing time to think about things?"

Darius studied Madalyn's face. She was even more beautiful than he remembered. He wasn't sure how that was possible, but he knew it to be true. This was the girl. The girl he'd fallen in love with all those years ago, the girl he'd planned to spend the rest of his life with. The girl he'd left with a broken heart. He pulled a deep breath into his lungs then pushed it back out again. "I do know something about that, yes."

"It takes as long as it takes."

Darius dipped his chin in silent agreement but kept his eyes on her face.

The microwave dinged, and Madalyn blinked. She hooked a finger around the edge of the plate and pulled it closer to where she sat. "You have a beer or two in there, Mol?"

Madalyn bit into one half of the sandwich and chewed while Darius watched her. Molly brought four bottles of beer to the island and popped the tops off them one at a time. She slid two of them toward Madalyn and gave one to her brother. The fourth she took for herself.

Darius began making a second sandwich, this time with mayo, while Madalyn ate. Neither one of them said anything, and the only sounds in the kitchen were the soft clang of dishes as Molly prepared a small bowl of potatoes which she placed on the island alongside a pitcher of gravy.

Finally, Madalyn finished the last bite of her sandwich and grabbed a napkin from the holder that sat on the counter. After a while, she reached over and began spooning some of the potatoes onto her plate. She made a valley in the center of the mound before pouring a hefty puddle of gravy into it.

"Two things that should always go together," she said, almost to herself.

Molly smiled before finishing off her beer. She set the bottle down and leaned against the counter. "Potatoes and gravy aren't the only two things that should always go together. You both came back," she said, first looking at her brother, then moving her gaze over to Madalyn. "That makes me think I'm not the only one who knows it."

The Gift of Music
A Personal Essay
July 15, 2016

I grew up a musician's daughter. Any time the subject of music comes up, my father comes attached. All of my very first memories have music in them ... a soundtrack of my life if you will. My father was talented; gifted at not only playing the guitar and singing, but at song writing as well. Perhaps he unknowingly planted the seed of storytelling deep inside me. He was a creative man. Mean as the devil and just as hot tempered, but creative as hell. I won't thank him for sharing his love of the written word. If it was a gift he gave me, let me reassure you, it wasn't given intentionally.

As hard as being my father's daughter always was for me, there is something I took away from our tumultuous twenty-one years together that I will always be grateful for. Out of all the memories I have of my dad ... not one of them that has anything at all to do with music is a bad one. Music was the only thing he and I agreed on. Music was the only thing we could easily share. Music was the only good bond the two of us ever had.

I don't know how succinct some of my very first memories are. The details are a little fuzzy with some of them, but I remember going to listen to my dad play in a band when I was very, very young. I had to be younger than five because I was with my mom at the time, and my parents divorced before I began first grade.

I recall with the utmost clarity the house we lived in when I was that age. It was a green house with two enormously tall pine trees at the end and on either side of the front walkway. There was a large, snowball bush to the side of the drive, its green leaves full of rounded spherical flowers made of tiny mint green petals that fell to the ground like a summertime snow shower.

The steps that led up to the wide porch were cement, all except the top one. It was wooden, just like the porch itself, and there was an overhang that I once raked my shin on so badly that tears immediately sprang to my eyes and blood poured from my torn skin down into my sock. I was following my dad into the house when it happened, me running to keep up with him and hitting the step in just the wrong way. When he turned and gruffly asked what was the matter, I remember shaking my head and telling him, "Nothing" before closing myself behind the bathroom door to nurse my wounds without his scrutiny.

The house was built in 1920, and my parents rented it from a man who had since moved out of state. Years after my parents divorced, my dad bought the property. It sat on half an acre of land; overgrown, wild and wonderful for a small child to play in. There was a tall tree that shaded the back. It dropped tiny, tart green apples from its boughs, and there were cherry trees we picked fruit from in a fenced off area at the far end of the land. One day I will write a book about that yard.

A lot of bad memories still live in that house on Bradburn Boulevard ... but there are a few boxes of good times tucked away for me there, too. The carpet was gray and thin, and the windows were tall, letting in a lot of buttery tinted sunshine. There was a big square of stained glass in the front window made by a friend of my parents' when I was very young. There was a broken pane; a jagged mistake in an otherwise beautifully choreographed piece of colors and shapes. It was left there when my dad, in one of his countless drunken rages, got angry with my mom and threw his keys. I don't know if they were thrown at her and he missed, or if he was aiming for the window. Nonetheless, I remember the scar his anger left there.

From the front door you could look straight through the house to the back; the living room, then the dining room on the left, two bedrooms and a bathroom on the right. The kitchen was a bright, sunny space my mom painted a happy combination of bold orange and yellow with a built-in eating nook tucked into one side.

One of the most memorable places in the house was the corner of the dining room. It didn't hold a table or any chairs. In fact, the only pieces of furniture there at all were an elaborate stereo and a set of powerful speakers. There in a semi-circle stacked against the walls were easily a hundred or more albums, all easy to flip through in order to find the one you wanted to listen to. Also in this space were several guitars laying in black cases lined in orange and red felt. This was a happy place. It was really the only happy place my dad and I shared.

I remember hearing about John Lennon's death in December 1980. I was nine years old. I'd grown up on the Beatles and knew exactly who John Lennon was. I've listened to and enjoyed them my entire life ... even had posters of them on my wall as an older teen, and I've always been quite fond of Paul McCartney and Wings. I had a good friend in high school who used to sing Beatles songs with me all the time. "Ob-la-di, Ob-la-da" was a particular favorite of ours back then. It's still one of my favorite songs today.

My dad was a huge fan of Elvis Presley, too.

He bought me "Elvis Golden Records", a two-album set of many of the King's greatest hits. I remember singing "All Shook Up" and "Teddy Bear", dancing around that long stretch of living/dining room on that gray carpet in my stocking feet. I made a reference to Elvis in my first novel, The Color of Thunder. There is a lot about my dad in that book. Elvis is one of the good parts.

There was the Steve Miller Band, Poco, The Who and The Rolling Stones. Steely Dan, Grateful Dead, Cheap Trick, Santana and Supertramp. Queen, Fleetwood Mac, Van Morrison and The Cars. I listened to Blondie, The Bee Gees, Tom Petty and the Heartbreakers, and one particular song, "Werewolves of London" by Warren Zevon that my father especially liked. Kansas, Billy Joel, Dire Straits and Elton John. He introduced me to "Sweet Home Alabama" by Lynyrd Skynard, and I remember how he loved listening to "You're the One That I Want" from the Grease soundtrack because he found the piano in that track so appealing. The list of artists and songs we listened to together goes on and on and on.

One of my favorite dad/music memories is him playing with his band Freeway. He played at the Goodsport Lounge most weekends, and I always looked forward to going. I can't remember exactly how old I was—somewhere between the ages of seven and ten I think—when he played with this group. Weekends were an event for me back then. My parents were divorced, and I opted to spend most of my time with my mom. I did enjoy going to the Goodsport, though. I felt right in my element there somehow. My dad was singing, playing his guitar, and I knew all the words to every song he played, even the ones that weren't appropriate for a younger child to know. I had a younger stepbrother whom I adored. He was four years my junior, and I would take him out on the dance floor and we would jump and dance and run around. We always sat in a circular booth right on the edge of the dance floor. We'd eat enormous cheeseburgers and a ton of fries and drink Cokes with a heap of sugary cherries in them. When one or two o'clock am would roll around, the band would pack up and the crowd would disperse. I was shaken awake and escorted, sleepy-eyed and exhausted, back to the car for our ride home. Was it the best environment for kids our age? I don't know. Maybe. Maybe not. All I know was that it was an absolute blast.

Anyone who knows me at all knows how much I love Duran Duran. Guess who introduced them to me? Yep. My dad. D2 released their album Rio in 1982. I was eleven at the time, and I had no idea who they were. My dad was a night owl who played his music loudly at all hours of the night. One early, early morning, I was awoken by a song that he was playing on repeat. It happened to be "Hungry Like the Wolf", and that was my first introduction to the band. About a year later, Duran Duran became my favorite band for all kinds of reasons; most of which are too hard to explain. Yes, I found them to be very attractive ... I was twelve at the time ... and I did use every picture of them I could find to wallpaper my walls and ceiling. It mostly had to do with the lyrics of their songs. I wrote a lot of poetry of my own back then. I used their music as a form of therapy to help me through some rough times during my pre-teen and teenage years. Duran Duran is still my most favorite band today, (although I haven't collected pictures of them for at least the past quarter of a century.) I was so excited to learn that they were playing Red Rocks this past September, (a venue they'd never played together as a group before) and there I was; back in Colorado again and able to go see them.

I grew up in the 70's and 80's ... and I love so much of the music that came from those decades. Chicago, Pretenders, Boston, Genesis, Eagles, Journey, Aerosmith, Van Halen, Thompson Twins, Howard Jones, INXS, Adam Ant, Laura Brannigan, The Doobie Brothers ... there's no way I can include them all here because there are just too many of them.

So much of the music from the 70's gets a serious head shake now, and I have always been embarrassed to admit to one of my most favorite songs because of that. I'll admit to it now. It's "Brandy" by Looking Glass. I'm not sure why I love it so much, or why I get a good feeling every time I hear it. Whatever memory I have attached to it is elusive ... it could be my dad, but I really don't know.

It wasn't until recently when a good friend of mine told me he thought it was one of the best love songs ever written that I decided I was going to own up to my fondness for it. Is it cheesy? Quite possibly, but it's still on my short list of songs I absolutely adore.

I love 90's stuff, too, and current music as well. I'm lucky that a lot of my favorite groups from when I was younger are making new albums right now, (that would include Duran Duran and Rick Springfield, whose album Rocket Science, released in early 2016, is one I listen to nearly every day.)

Rick Springfield, coincidentally, is also my dad's fault. Springfield's album Living in Oz was another one both of us loved and listened to together.

One of my more recent favorites is Big Bad Voodoo Daddy. They started up in 1989, but I didn't hear them until about 2008. They're called a contemporary swing revival band, and they cover artists such as Cab Calloway and Bennie Goodman. They make me want to dance. I have a really hard time listening to BBVD without moving. They are my happy, feel good music. I welcome happy, feel good music. Everyone needs a hearty helping of that in their lives.

I love Broadway musicals and jazz, I love listening to piano and classical. I even enjoy country. I like harder stuff, too, although it's not necessarily my favorite. (I did say I grew up in the 80's, didn't I? Hairbands galore... oh, yes, and AC/DC and all that amazing classic rock.) New music is wonderful, too. I'm introduced to a plethora of current artists via my seventeen-year-old daughter and my almost daily perusal of Spotify. I enjoy so much.

I know this post was supposed to be an easy one. It was most likely meant to be fun and simple, but music isn't any of those things for me. It never has been. Music, to me, is my dad. It's the very best part of my dad. It's the only part I want to keep hold of. Music, just like the relationship he and I shared, is anything but easy or simple.

After many, many years of an incredibly difficult and painful relationship, I decided to estrange myself from my dad and that side of my family. I was not quite twenty-one years old when I did that. Eight years later, on August 19, 2000 he died of a heart attack. He was only fifty-two years old. I don't know the details surrounding his demise. I heard that he'd suffered one attack that put him in the hospital, then a second one that killed him, but that's only from second-hand knowledge. That was nearly sixteen years ago, but the time I spent with him, the experiences I had with him and because of him are all still fresh in my head and in my heart.

This post was supposed to be about the music I love. I didn't write about the details of the incredibly dysfunctional and abusive relationship I had with my father for various reasons ... but I did take advantage of this topic in order to unburden myself of thoughts I've been carrying around of him lately. Even though I haven't spoken to him in twenty-four years, I think of him almost daily ... and I can't write about the subject of music without also writing about him. They are tightly linked, the two of them, and they always will be.

Shortly before our estrangement I learned that my dad was converting his garage into a recording studio. I'd heard a few of the songs he was planning to record. One of them was about having too many chiefs and not enough Indians. I've since looked it up, curious to find out whether or not he'd actually made an album. Seems to me that I heard somewhere that he had, but if that's true, I wasn't able to find it. I did, however, find a couple of other songs about chiefs and Indians; one recorded by Brant Bjork and another by Dean Martin. I remember listening to (and enjoying) the song my dad wrote and know that, while the titles are the same, his was an original. My dad believed himself to be a chief, and those around him were Indians.

My father was a really difficult human being ... dominant and scary and so many other awful things ... but he did have exceptional taste in music. He knowingly shared his love for it with me, and for that I owe him my thanks.

Reflections

The water, so calm
the night, so warm
The stars are on the water
and a cricket's chirp in the air

A soft breeze, and a breath
A quiet lull in the night
and a sense of loneliness
sits in the air

Soft cattails whisper
in the wind
A soft, cottony dandelion
And a small sigh from the grass

A light bug skips over the water
leaving a trail of gold dust
A small hum
then silence

A leaf, like a sailboat
on a journey in the water
A small sail with a crew
of crickets and ladybugs

A rustle in the trees
A noise in the grass
A waterfall over the rocks
and a cold stream on the shore

A reflection of blue eyes,
of strong thoughts
and a smile

play with the water

The moonlight slips through
and there you are
right behind me
in a serious trance

And with a sigh
A gentle breeze
there's a ripple and a wave
and you're gone.

8/17/87

Letter to an Inanimate Object

Dear Couch,

I have mixed feelings about you, truth be told. We have a lot of history, you and me. As I lie reading on you this early morning before the sun was even awake, a lot of memories popped into my head. Because of this, I decided there were a few things I needed to let you know.

We first met back in January of 2012. My family and I were new to Germany and had just moved into a rather large home. It was beautiful–lots of windows and a huge expanse of bright, white tile on the floors. It was a little uncomfortable at first, though. All our belongings were packed away in a big, blue container that was on a ship bobbing around somewhere on the vast Atlantic Ocean. The few folding chairs we'd borrowed and the hearth in the living room were the only places for us to sit, so when we met you we were all very happy indeed.

You were hanging out at the Poco. I'm sure you remember it although you haven't been there in almost five years. It's a wonderful store right in the heart of Kaiserslautern. It has three floors just stuffed with all sorts of things a family who has just moved into a large, empty house needs. I'd like to say it was love at first sight, but that wouldn't be entirely accurate. There was another couch there, a leather one that caught our eye as well. After much debate, we realized that the wonderfully wide windowsills in our new house required a couch with a shorter back. The leather one simply wouldn't fit, so we decided to take you home.

This, I'm afraid, is where our troubles began. Perhaps this wasn't all your fault, although you do weigh an awful lot. Even with all your parts separated, you are a mighty heavy haul. It didn't help that we had to climb two flights of stairs—made of stone and covered in ice that time of the year—just to get to our front door. After that, there was a large, spiral staircase we had to conquer inside the house before we were able to reach the living room. I think I recall moving a couple of your rather weighty pieces around the back of the house to avoid that second set of stairs. All I remember was mud, some very thorny bushes and a gate we couldn't open. I think I've blocked the rest of that adventure out of my mind. I will say that once we got you into the house and in front of the fireplace where you belonged, you looked mighty nice. And we were grateful for a place to sit down since all four of us were exhausted and a bit battered from moving you in.

The living room didn't look quite so big once you arrived. You were accommodating, serving as not only a place to sit or lie down, but as a dinner table and a place to complete school work. Perhaps the fact that you were so useful for a considerable amount of time is why those feelings I mentioned earlier are mixed. You see, I'm an optimist. The glass is always half full. Perhaps in this case, the cushions are always half plumped. Well, maybe not. Anyway, I'm confident you see the point I'm trying to make here.

Having said that, however, we need to face the harsh reality. You're big. You're bulky. Sometimes you're simply in the way. How many times have we all stubbed our toes on your pointed corners? I know that my left pinkie toe will never be the same since you reached out and grabbed me that one cold November day back in 2013. I'm not as sure of the other dates in which you caused my family or me bodily injury, but you have a rap sheet at least as long as your middle fold out section filled with your misdemeanors and acts of random violence.

I thought maybe your crime spree would end once we all relocated back to the States, but you proved to be an international criminal. Not even the burly trio of professional movers escaped harm at your hands—er wood frame and upholstery. The exact nature of their injuries was never revealed, but I know I saw at least one of them limp out the door once you were safely inside, and the string of profanities that filled the house while they were moving you in makes it a certainty that you were the cause.

When we brought you up to the living room a year and a half ago, you pulled off your most heinous crime to date. While I'd had lots of issues with my wrist before you came upstairs, it was this last move that finally did it in. Just a week after the kids and I got you situated in your final spot, I began seeing an orthopedic surgeon. It was decided that wielding your heft was the straw that broke the camel's back. Or more specifically, the joint in my wrist. It was with much bitterness that I curled up beneath a blanket on your less than comfortable surface and lay my head upon your misshapen cushions after several painful cortisone shots and two difficult surgeries. I'd come to terms with the fact that you were not the nicest piece of furniture we'd ever owned, but you'd finally gone too far.

You've been with us for five years, so you might be wondering why I'm writing this letter to you now. I did mention before that I was trying to get a little reading done this morning. I don't do that very often. As a matter of fact, you may have noticed that you and I don't spend a whole lot of time together lately. My toes are afraid of you, and quite honestly, you're just not pleasant to hang around with. My attempt at finishing a book today just reminded me of that, and that's why I felt the need to vent.

Truly, I hate to hurt your feelings, but it's past time that I tell you if we hadn't bought you in Germany, and if we could afford to buy a new couch here, you'd be history. Oh, and that little incident after my last wrist surgery ... you know, the one where my belly decided it didn't like all the meds the surgeon pumped into me? I'm not at all sorry. Consider it payback.

Sincerely,
The person who would rather watch T.V. and read on the floor

My Dad and Elvis Presley
A Personal Essay
January 8, 2018

Today would have been Elvis Presley's eighty-third birthday, had he lived. There are some conspiracy theorists out there who say he is alive. I don't know anything about that. I do know that if my dad was here, he would have celebrated his seventieth birthday back in November. There are no theories about the man who was my father. Everyone agrees that he has, in fact, left the building.

In spirit, though, my dad is very much alive. At least for me he is. It's just kind of understood that parents are a huge part of their children's lives. How could it possibly be any different? No one talks about it, it's just a fact. It's the way things are. Even though this is something that isn't questioned, it still amazes me on a surprisingly frequent basis just how much influence parents continue to have on the lives of their kids—even after those kids become adults themselves, and a long, long time after those parents are gone.

I was never a Daddy's girl. I wanted to be. Oh, lord, how I wanted to be. I think every little girl does. That wasn't the kind of relationship my dad and I had, though. The two of us weren't anything alike, not from the very beginning. For one, I'm a girl. After he finally came to terms with the fact that he was going to be a father, I had the audacity to be born female. That didn't come as too much of a shock for my grandfather who had four daughters of his own, my mother included. I've heard a story about how he took the news of my arrival. "Of course she's a girl," he said. "I never expected anything else." It was a joke that my grandpa had started to doubt that we'd have any little boys born into the family. That wasn't a joke my dad found very funny.

There were other reasons he didn't like me much. Even at the start, it was obvious that the two of us had different personalities. I'm soft … both in heart and with my words, he was gruff both physically and verbally. I'm playful, but he teased mercilessly. I'm affectionate, but he liked to use open palms and clenched fists. We were like oil and water.

He was different around other people. He was funny and engaging, and women loved him. Things were better for us when we were with a crowd. He gathered up all his good qualities and showed them off when we weren't alone. It took me a long time to realize that he was carrying a lot of his own pain and anger inside him. Even after years and years of dealing with his substance abuse and counseling, both with him and on my own, that still wasn't clear to me. He never talked about it. Never shared. He's been gone for seventeen years now. I've learned a lot about him that I didn't know back then, and I see it now. I realize how good he was at hiding that pain and anger when in the presence of those outside his family.

My dad was a good-looking guy, and when he smiled, I remember feeling hopeful. It was a good smile, a striking smile, and I loved seeing it on his face. I see him in me when I look in the mirror. We don't look a lot alike, but I carry much of him with me. His hair was wavy and dark. His eyes were hazel, but most people thought they were brown. You had to get really close to him to see the green and gold that swirled inside them. I got his big, wide eyes. I was gifted his long eyelashes, too, but not his prominent Greek nose. Although my Dutch ancestry gave me fair skin, blonde hair, and blue-green eyes, my dad peers out at me sometimes when I let him. My smile? He only gets partial credit for that. My mom has a pretty killer smile of her own.

I may not have been a Daddy's girl, and the two of us might not have had much in common ... but he unknowingly gave me something I could relate to, something that came from him that was good in every single way. Music. And that's where Elvis comes in.

It would take me a very long time to list all the music my dad introduced me to. He was born in 1947, so he listened to all of the amazing songs that came out of the 50s, 60s, 70s and 80s. My mom liked music, but she didn't have a passion for it like my dad did. He was a musician himself, and he played in a few bands while I was growing up. The one I remember the most was called Freeway, and he played lead guitar and sang lead vocals in the smoky, dimly lit Goodsport Lounge while my younger step-brother and I bounced and ran around the dance floor until we couldn't keep our eyes open any longer. We ate many cheeseburgers and drank countless Cokes in that rounded, red vinyl booth—the same one we'd crawl into when the clock crawled past midnight and we could dance no more.

My dad converted a corner of the dining room into his music space. He had rows and rows of albums lined up against the walls. I'd sit on that gray, threadbare carpet, and I'd go through the stacks to see the artwork on all the covers. It didn't matter how many times I'd seen them, I always wanted to look at them again. He had several guitars, and the cases would always be opened, a cat or two curled up in the red or bright orange felt that covered the insides. Music was always playing, and I knew the words to all the songs. Like I said, I couldn't possibly include every album that spun on that turntable, but the two artists that had the most profound effect on me were undoubtedly the Beatles and Elvis Presley.

It didn't matter that my dad and I had been haphazardly thrown together in this life, completely mismatched and unsuited for one another while we sat in that corner of his house on Bradburn Boulevard. Whoever was in charge of making sure parents got the right babies screwed up big time when it came to him and me … but all of that was forgotten in that dining room corner with music swirling around us.

He never scolded me while we were there together. He never told me not to touch the albums. He never made me feel self-conscious when I'd get up and dance. He never made me feel less than. He never made me feel stupid, or ugly, or wrong. I never felt the shock of his hand against my skin … and his smile was nearly as bright as the sunshine coming through those tall windows. He shared something he loved with me—something he loved with all his heart and soul—and it became a part of me. It's a part I will always love. A part that I am incredibly grateful for. A part that has gotten me through some of the most difficult times in my life.

There were many Elvis albums, but the one I remember the most was Elvis' Golden Records. "Hound Dog", "All Shook Up", "Jailhouse Rock", Too Much", "Don't Be Cruel", "Treat Me Nice" … oh, so many wonderful songs. I loved that album so much that my dad bought me my own copy for Christmas, but I liked listening to it with him best. He had a terrific voice, and he sang right along with the King. It was marvelous, and to this day, every time I hear Elvis, these incredible music sessions with my father come to mind.

One summer day when I was six, I was sitting beside my dad in his Dodge van. We'd just come back from doing something—what I can't recall—and the radio was on. He'd just pulled the van into the driveway when we heard the news that Elvis had died. I didn't realize that he'd only been forty-two years old at the time, or how incredibly young that was. I didn't know the particulars surrounding his death, and at six, I didn't think to ask. What affected me the most was my father's reaction to the news. It blindsided him. He was speechless. I remember watching him as he stared at the radio, and I had to blink, then squint when I thought I detected a tear in his eye. I'd never seen my dad cry before. He was all bluster and mean, scary words spoken in a loud, angry voice. His emotion was heated and fearful … not sad and thoughtful. That's a memory that will forever be wedged into my head.

So, on what would have been Elvis' eighty-third birthday, I find myself listening to many of the songs my dad introduced me to, and feeling grateful that, even though he didn't mean to, he gave me a beautiful, irreplaceable gift. It's one I hold near and dear to my heart, and something that I enjoy nearly every day of my life.

Cold Feet

The Groom

The church smelled of wax and roses. Suffocating, although I seemed to be the only one who thought so. I felt too warm, too restricted wrapped up in this expensive monkey suit. There were far too many buttons, too many shiny, uncomfortable poky bits, and this bow tie ... what was up with this damn torture device anyway? I reached up and tugged on it, only to have Amanda pull my hand away and look up at me with her squinted, hazel eyes. I parted my lips but kept my teeth clamped together.

"It's too tight," I hissed.

"Stop fidgeting or I'll make you hold my hand like I did when we were little."

The truth was, Amanda had always been little. The top of her head barely reached my shoulder, and she weighed just over a hundred pounds. Still, she was a force to be reckoned with, and normally I would listen and comply when she gave an order. Now she was issuing a threat, one she thought would stop my somewhat childish behavior, but I wanted to move and pull at my bowtie even more after I heard her words in the desperate hope that she'd follow through with her punishment.

I scanned the room and realized that it was full. There were easily two hundred guests if not more sitting in the nave of the church. I shook my head. Who in the hell knows this many people? I certainly didn't.

The pews were separated by a center aisle. On one side sat a collection of individuals that were in some way either related to me by blood or attached by some other means. I squinted. Okay, that guy, the older one, the one sitting next to Aunt Audrey. What's his name? He's the guy who packages up Mom's pork chops and freshly ground beef over at Simpson's Market every Saturday. I realized I had never seen him dressed in anything other than the blood-stained, yellowing apron he always wore wrapped around his round, Santa Claus belly. He wasn't related, but he had supplied the main course of every meal served on my mother's dinner table since as far back as I could remember. Nothing says family like a neatly trimmed pork roast.

Wait. It's coming to me. Mr. Gregory. Yes, that's his name. Memories of Mom greeting him with a smile on her face as I tagged along with her as a child on her weekly shopping trips poked at my over addled brain. They were gone as quickly as they'd appeared.

I reached up and pulled the collar of my shirt away from my neck so that I could swallow down the horrid taste that had accumulated on the back of my tongue. I couldn't help but notice that Mr. Gregory looked wildly out of place in his fancy pin-striped suit and silk tie. Almost as out of place as I felt.

"Stop it, Caleb." Amanda reached up and gave the sleeve of my jacket a hard tug. "I mean it." Her voice was a whisper, but I heard it loud and clear. She'd been talking to me for years. Now I wish I had been better at listening.

I turned my head and looked at the assortment of people I'd never seen before seated on the other side of the aisle. My eyes scanned the rows of well-dressed guests. The longer I looked, the faster my heart seemed to beat. I was beginning to panic. I needed to find someone, anyone I recognized.

Finally, my gaze landed on two people who looked vaguely familiar. James and Alex, my soon to be brothers-in-law. James sat still, his hands in his lap. It was obvious the kid was bored, but he was politely so, just as he'd been taught. I spied the cords trailing from the buds in Alex's ears. They were attached to his phone, which had undoubtedly been snuck into the church. A quiet rebel, that one. He was looking at me, his mouth moving, but the words he silently spoke were not meant for me. By the way he bobbed his head, my guess was that he wasn't listening to a ballad. The tempo to his unheard song was at least as fast as the pounding of my heart.

My stomach clenched. Yes, I'd seen these two before. I'd even spent some time with them. Still, I didn't know them any better today than I had months ago when we'd first been introduced. Seeing them now made me feel worse instead of better, and I nearly jumped when the first few notes of the wedding march sounded.

I looked away from the boys and took in a huge breath of waxy, floral scented air. Everyone in the pews shifted toward the center aisle, and like a wave on the ocean, all heads turned and looked at the back of the room.

There she was, my bride, all dressed in white. Her head was covered in the filmy netting of an intricate veil, and her neck was draped in a single strand of pearls. I watched as she walked toward me, the skirt of her full gown swinging forward and back like a large, silent bell with each step she took.

She held onto her father's arm as he escorted her down the aisle. Funny, I thought, as I scrutinized the man walking beside her. How come I hadn't realized until now just how big and formidable he is? Then I realized it wasn't funny at all.

The notes from the organ seemed to swell in the overheated, over scented room. The space was large, but I felt boxed in, like I was being crowded and deprived of air. My bride continued to make her way toward me, her steps timed perfectly, just like she'd practiced at rehearsal.

In another few seconds, she was standing right in front of me, the organist timing the conclusion of the oft played piece of music with my bride's last approaching steps.

"Who gives this woman to be married to this man?"

"Her mother and I do."

Again, just as we'd practiced, I reached to take the edge of the white, tulle veil she wore between my clumsy fingers. The room was hushed, the only sounds filling the silence were the swishing of wedding programs as they were used to fan heated faces.

"You're crazy," I thought to myself. "So dramatic."

I felt a spark of confidence return to urge me on and I took a deep breath. I smiled as I slowly lifted the fabric up and over my bride's head. That's when I knew I'd been right to be so ill at ease.

The face I uncovered didn't belong to the woman I truly wanted to marry.

The Bride

Mama fussed over me, making sure the long line of tiny buttons climbing up my back were all fastened correctly. She hummed to herself as she fluffed, folded, straightened, adjusted then readjusted.

I imagined I was much like any bride, decorated like a beautiful cake and made to stand still while all the frosting and other sparkly things were placed until they were just so.

I'd waited a long time for this. Today I was the diamond, and I was going to shine, shine, shine.

Daddy had gone through this past week acting tough and manly like always. A man of few words, he shook hands and engaged in brief and awkward looking hugs when greeting out of town guests. He can't fool me, though. He tries to hide them, but I have always been able to find his vulnerable spots. I'm his little girl. Those spots are there because I gave them to him.

The sun was shining brightly in the hall when Mama and I walked out. She kept telling me not to cry, not to ruin my make up while she dabbed at her own eyes with a smudged tissue. Daddy was there, a close-mouthed smile hiding beneath his neatly trimmed mustache. He was a big man, handsomely dressed in his black tuxedo. Before Mama lowered the veil over my face I thought I saw that his eyes were looking a little red, too. I just smiled up at him without saying a word. He wasn't on the verge of tears. It was dust, I'm sure, or the pollen swirling around in the summer time air.

I saw Daddy move his elbow away from his body and I slipped my arm inside. His hand was warm when it covered mine, and I leaned into him.

"You're beautiful, baby girl."

I smiled. Yes. The pollen sure was thick this morning.

My heels clicked along the tiled hall. Mama pressed a kiss to my cheek before she slipped between the big double doors and disappeared inside. In a few moments, she would be sitting in the first pew, and it would be time for the wedding to begin.

It had taken awhile for us to get to this point. To say Mama and Daddy had not been excited about me marrying Caleb Graysen would be an understatement.

Mama never denied the fact that Caleb was handsome. His hair, the color of mahogany, and his eyes, a light green framed by dark lashes, were an appealing combination. She'd mentioned once or twice that the two of us would have beautiful babies someday—if that was what I wanted, of course, to have babies with someone other than the handful of worthy suitors she and Daddy had been suggesting over the years. Mama never argued Caleb's well-mannered demeanor, either. Even though he'd never traveled further south than Oklahoma City, he always remembered to say yes or no ma'am. She wasn't completely won over, but she wasn't completely opposed to our union. Caleb had charmed her just as he'd charmed me.

Daddy, however, was a different story.

Caleb wasn't good enough for his little girl. Caleb didn't have enough money, or a well-known, highly respected family lineage. He thought Caleb was soft. He never used the word spineless, but I know it had crossed his mind a time or two. The fact that Caleb wasn't incredibly fond of whiskey … well, that didn't help much, either.

Then there was that whole thing about Caleb asking his best friend, Amanda Martin, to stand up with him at the wedding. Mama couldn't get past the fact that he had chosen a best woman instead of a man. It was untraditional. Didn't he have any brothers or a cousin somewhere who would do him the honor? Daddy thought it unnatural that a man would have a female best friend. They had been best friends, though, since childhood. It was something Caleb felt strongly about, having Amanda up at the altar with him, and it was one of the things I knew I would not be able to talk him out of.

My parents didn't understand what it was that I found so intriguing about Caleb Graysen. I could see where they were coming from. He wasn't the kind of boy I'd been attracted to in the past. He was not all that interested in sports, but he'd pretended to be knowledgeable in tennis when we first met. It was obvious that he'd never picked up a racket when I finally got him on the court, although the black eye he sported for more than a week after I accidently hit him with a ball was somewhat endearing. He had no interest in watching football or television or playing eighteen holes with Daddy at the club.

His clothes were something else. I'd called him slovenly many times in the past. He thought the term harsh and inadequate, and defended his blue jeans and soft button-down shirts as acceptably comfortable.

Being well-dressed was not the only thing Caleb shunned. He was also quite helpless with social interaction. He fumbled over small talk and had only lived outside of the small town in which he was raised since attending university five years ago. Fortunately, his nose was always stuck in a book. He'd filled his head with things he'd never experienced, traveled to places he'd never seen, and lived a multitude of lives he'd never lived. He had a college degree on which to stand, and he held his own, although the tight smiles my friends wore on their faces while we were all out for the evening told me they talked meanly about Caleb behind his back.

There was that stain on his favorite sweatshirt that drove me crazy, and his hair always seemed just a little too long. He wore sneakers all the time, and his dog liked to sit with him on the couch. Heath wasn't the worst dog in the world. He was sweet, but he was big and hairy, and he slobbered. A lot. And why did he have to go everywhere Caleb went?

I cleared my throat as Daddy moved me closer to the doors. The organist had not yet begun to play, and I felt the grip I had on my bouquet slip. The palms of my hands felt sweaty, and I was finding it hard to breathe from beneath my veil.

I heard them, the first notes of the wedding march, and I saw Daddy look over at me out of the corner of my eye. He patted my hand again before pressing his palm against the door. When he pushed it open, I felt a rush of warm air pour over me, the scent of wax and roses hovering around my covered head. Everyone in the room turned in one fluid motion. Their eyes were all on me.

Shine, shine, shine.

I wanted to wipe my sweaty palm on the full skirt of my dress, but I didn't. I wrapped my fingers tightly around the handle of my bouquet and took a step.

Pause. Step. Pause.

As I passed each pew, I saw people smiling at me. There were murmurs as I moved. "Such a beautiful bride!" "What an extraordinary dress!" "Those flowers are stunning!" These whispers carried me to the front of the church, and all the while I ignored the gnawing I felt down deep in my gut.

Cold feet. That's all it is. Just cold feet.

I heard a male voice. The pastor. Then Daddy was speaking. I looked to the side, saw him smile at me again before he sat down next to Mama. When I turned, I was facing Caleb.

He reached out and took the edges of my veil in his fingers. Was he shaking? The gnawing in my belly grew worse as he lifted the lace and tulle. When he moved the veil over the top of my head, I caught his gaze.
Not cold feet.

I knew in that instant that Caleb did not want to marry me.

What surprised me even more than that, though, was the realization that I didn't want to marry him, either.

Amanda

Caleb turned and looked at me, a sheen in his green eyes. I took a deep breath and smiled at him. It's taken him years to see it, but it looks like Caleb finally figured out that I'm the best woman—at least the best woman for him—after all.

Time Traveling Taxi

Car trouble. I sighed. I hadn't had a meeting scheduled in ... well ... years. Of course, it would happen like this. The one day I needed to be somewhere, and here I was. Stuck.

I pulled my phone from my pocket and did some quick research before calling a local cab company. The last time I'd needed a taxi, things hadn't gone so well. I crossed my fingers and hoped for the best.

It took less than ten minutes for the driver to find me. I was surprised when the car pulled up. It was a classic yellow Checker cab from the fifties, complete with a pair of broad shoulders, huge bumpers and the silver hood emblem I'd seen so many times in movies.

The passenger side window was rolled down and I bent to peer in. The driver wore a white t-shirt, the sleeves folded tight against his biceps, and had a cigarette hanging out of his mouth. He grinned and tossed his thumb toward the backseat. "C'mon, baby. Climb in. We need to beat feet."

I stood on the curb and blinked at him. Then I straightened up and looked around my cul-de-sac. What year was this? I was sure the cabbie had a New York accent, although we were smack dab in the middle of the mid-west. Looking back into the car I saw him grin at me, the cigarette still hanging between his lips. He gave me a bit of a Danny Zuko vibe. It was a little freaky, but I'd always kind of liked John Travolta, so I shrugged and got into the back seat.

"This address is downtown," I told him scrolling through my phone again.

"Don't worry about it," he said.

"What do you mean, don't worry about it?" I caught the reflection of his eyes in the rearview mirror. "I need to get to this meeting. That's why I called you."

"Mellow out," the cabbie told me. "Things are copacetic. Sit back, relax and let me take you for a ride. I'll get you to the only meeting that matters."

He swung the big car around, and I slid a little in my seat as I watched his eyes in the mirror. I was about to open my mouth again to argue when the scenery outside the windows began to blur. I felt a surge of speed as the car lurched forward, and my head was pressed against the seat. My mouth remained agape, but no words found their way past my lips.

The mileage tracker on the dashboard began to spin, and I watched it as the car continued to rush forward. It took me a moment to realize that it wasn't keeping track of the distance we traveled but was displaying the date instead. Just like in Back to The Future, the digital readout skipped past months, days and years. I watched it as the world outside the windows whirled by. According to the read out, we were going back in time.

Great Scott. This was heavy.

2012, 2007, 2002 …

"Uh, Danny?" I asked, reaching up to thread my fingers in the wire mesh that separated me from the driver. "What the hell is going on?"

He tipped his head and looked at me in the mirror again. His hands were on the wheel, and his foot was pressed down on the gas pedal.

"There's a chick needs some advice. You'll recognize her when you see her."

"What?" I asked. "What are you talking about?"

2000, 1997, 1994 ...

"The only one who can talk to her is you. You dig what I'm sayin'?"

I shook my head. "No," I told him, my voice rising to be heard over the sound of wind passing over the car. I didn't know if it was wind I was hearing, but I did know that it felt as if we were moving incredibly fast. There were objects outside the windows, but we passed by them too quickly for me to make any of them out. "I definitely don't dig what you're saying. Just what is it that you're trying to tell me?"

1992, 1991 ...

The car was slowing down. I watched the display as it clicked to May 1990. Then it stopped. Danny pulled the taxi into what looked like a parking lot, and I peered out of the windows trying to see where we'd wound up.

"Oh, wow ..." I said, catching sight of a place I'd passed many hours in while growing up. "I haven't been here in a long time."

Danny parked the cab and turned off the engine. "That thing doesn't look too sturdy," He said, pointing through the windshield at a roller coaster across the street from where we were parked.

"That's Lakeside," I told him, my eyes following the wooden structure. "It opened way back in 1910 or something like that. I'm not sure, but I remember reading somewhere that they used to call it White City because of all the lights on that tower right there. If I'm honest, I'm surprised any of it is still standing."

"You been there?"

I nodded. "Lots of times. There used to be a fun house. There was this animatronic lady out front, standing way above the entrance. She was big. For some reason, I remember her wearing an orange dress." I brushed the thought away. "Any way, she stood up there and laughed. She laughed all day long. You could hear her from the other side of the park. There were these barrels inside. Three of them. They were huge, big enough that you could walk through them. The two on the outside spun in the same direction, but the one in the middle spun the opposite way."

I shifted in the seat and continued to stare at the skyline. "There were big metal slides in there. You rode down them, your knees on big squares of carpet, and there was this spinning ride. Everyone sat in the middle and the floor would spin, faster and faster. Kids would literally fly from the center and hit the outside fence because they couldn't stay put."

"Sounds like a gas," Danny said with a chuckle, the ashes from his cigarette falling into his lap.

"It was," I agreed. "Though I'm surprised more people didn't get hurt. I came out of there with a few bumps and bruises myself, that's for sure."

Danny motioned out the window with his dimpled chin. "That girl right there looks like she's got some bumps and bruises."

I followed his gaze and saw a young girl sitting on one of the black sling swings in the playground. My stomach did a flip as I studied her, and I blinked back the sudden onslaught of tears that filled my eyes. I meant to say something, but what came out of my mouth was more of a strangled cry than any semblance of words.

"You're the only one who can help her," he told me.

"But how? All the bad stuff is still going to happen to her ..." I shook my head. "I mean to me. A lot of it already has. I can't change history. It doesn't work that way, right?" I turned and stared at him. "I saw all three of those movies. I don't have a picture of myself handy, but if I did, the last thing I'd want to see is me fading away leaving nothing but background."

Danny took another drag from his cigarette, then blew out the smoke so it filled the front of his cab. "Who did you have back then?"

I watched the younger me, and the tears came to my eyes again. "No one."

"That's why we're here."

"Not to change things ..." my voice faded.

"You're the only one who knows exactly how she feels right now. You're the only one who knows exactly what's ahead of her. You can't move any of the stumbling blocks, but maybe you can help her navigate around them. Be who you needed back then."

I sniffed. "I'm asleep, right? Having one hell of a nightmare?" I searched his Travoltaesque face, but nothing I saw there helped answer my question. "This is the strangest thing I've ever experienced."

Danny blew a puff of smoke into my face. The scent made me light-headed for a moment, and I scooted away from him. He gave me a smile.

"Bug out," he said just as the back door of the cab opened, sending a rush of fresh, spring time air into the car. "I'll be here when you get back."

I tried to gather myself, then slid across the wide seat and pushed myself from the car. I looked up and saw pieces of the sky through the canopy of trees overhead. It was a bright and brilliant blue. That sky had always been one of my most favorite things about Colorado. When I looked forward again and saw the younger me on the swings, I knew on that day I hadn't noticed the beauty of the sky.

Filling my lungs with fresh air, I shut the car door and began to walk across the playground. I remembered the park well. I'd been here a million times. My dad had caught two enormous frogs by one of the banks and brought them home. They lived for years in a huge fish tank in his living room. Petey and Yellow Throat were slimy buggers, but they'd been appealing in their own way.

I'd learned to ride my bike here. I was a slow learner—nine by the time I'd gotten the hang of it—and we'd done some family fitness around this lake. My dad had been a runner and thought the rest of us should be, too. I remember jogging behind him, my step-brother complaining about how thirsty he was. "Swallow your spit," my dad would tell him. The complaining must have gotten to be too much for him eventually because I don't remember our running days around Berkeley Lake lasting very long.

On many an Independence Day we'd come to the park, situating ourselves as close to the main thoroughfare, the one that separated the grassy area of the park and the entrance to Lakeside, as we could. We spread blankets, ate from coolers and bought glow in the dark necklaces. After the sun went down, we'd watch as fireworks exploded above the unlit tower and the old, creaky frame of the Cyclone—the roller coaster that had both thrilled and terrified guests of the amusement park for decades.

There had been many lunches on the grass. I never remember my dad drinking soda except during our picnics. Then he enjoyed a can of Mountain Dew or two. When we were finished eating, I'd jump up and run to the playground.

I slowly walked toward the younger me who was dangling on a swing, my eyes moving over the equipment that had been set up in the gravel. It had been different when I was little. There was a huge cement frog squatting in the middle of the play area. He'd been at least double my height back then, his deep green paint worn so I could see the gray beneath it. He was a climbing frog, and when I got to the top, I'd slide back down along his back, or perch myself in the crook of one of his fat froggy legs.

The frog was gone now, replaced by something that looked like a seal. It had less character than the frog had, but even back then, my amphibian friend probably had some years on him. It had been a long time since I'd played on this playground.

My feet made noise in the pea gravel that filled the area. I walked slowly, remembering how at risk I'd felt on those mornings I'd driven to Berkeley Park. It had been my haven back then. It had been a place I thought no one would look for me. I'd been hiding from the world, and no one had ever found me.

This was such a strange circumstance, standing there, looking at me from twenty-six years ago. I studied the girl hanging in the swing wearing a pair of blue jeans and a sweatshirt. I couldn't see them, but I knew the longer sleeves hid the red marks that wrapped around her wrists.

Her hair was a unique blonde color, the result of a disastrous dye job done almost a year before. I remembered it well. I'd flown to Virginia and spent a month with an old friend. She'd mentioned how good my naturally dark blonde hair would look with a few highlights. She'd coated the long strands in a stinky goo, then wrapped it all up in a towel. An hour later I was standing in the mirror staring at a pale girl with hair so black it shone blue in the light. My friend claimed it had been a mistake. I didn't believe it back then. I'm still not convinced of it today.

I did a mental headshake. Her hair was the least of her problems right now.

"Hi." I tried to speak softly, but I still startled her.

She looked up and my heart broke. She wore her bangs long, but they swept off to the right side of her forehead and did a poor job of concealing the discoloration that was settling deep and dark around her left eye.

"Oh," she stammered. "Hey."

She blinked, and I stared at her smooth, nineteen-year-old face. Her eyes were so large, and I could see an oval shaped shadow of a bruise that colored the line of her jaw. Her bottom lip, normally full, was more so than usual. She'd covered it up with a dark lipstick, one she'd never liked because it was too red for her pale complexion, but she'd only been partially successful in covering the bruise he'd put there with his own mouth.

I wondered again how it was possible that no one had remarked on the beating, the physical proof that something had gone terribly wrong for her. I knew she'd seen members of her own family several times since that night, but no one, save her brother, had reacted to the difference in her appearance. She'd gone to work, to the store, to fill her car with gas. No one had said a single thing.

She needed someone to say something.

I glanced up to where the cab was parked. I couldn't see Danny from where I sat, but his words played in my head. "Be who you needed back then."

Taking a deep breath, I turned back to the girl. She had her arms wrapped around the chains of the swing and one hand holding onto her other wrist to keep from falling backward. The toes of her white Keds were stained brown. She wore no socks beneath the rolled cuffs of her jeans. I couldn't see her legs, but, just like her wrists, I knew there were marks there. Especially around her right ankle.

She squinted up at me. She had freckles across the bridge of her nose and on the swell of each cheek. I'd almost forgotten I'd ever had them. "You look familiar."

I nodded at her. "So do you." I moved forward a bit and reached out to grab the chain of the swing beside her. "Mind if I sit with you for a while?"

She didn't speak, just shook her head.

I wasn't sure how many days had passed since it happened, but it couldn't have been more than one or two. I'd gone back to school after that, but only to one class. The paper I'd been working on that night was due a week later. If it hadn't been a team project, I probably would've let it slide. My partner was counting on me, though, and I couldn't let her down.

The swing was tight around my hips as I sat down. I noticed that the younger me fit in hers just fine. Just one of the many things that had changed over the years.

"Listen," I began. "I know how badly you're hurting right now." She opened her mouth to protest, but I wouldn't let her speak. "I know better than anyone. Things are really messed up right now." I snorted softly. "That's not true," I corrected myself. "Things are horrible, but you're okay."

"I'm not."

I knew exactly what she was thinking. "You will be."

"What if—"

"There are no what if's," I interrupted. "Not as far as he's concerned. You left everything behind you in the house that night. Memories are all you have left. Don't worry about the rest."

She let out a shuddery sigh, and I saw a teardrop fall from her lashes. That knowledge would have been a gift to me back then. Long after I'd physically healed, I still carried the fear that what he'd done to me in that bedroom had the power to ruin so much of my future.

"It hurts like hell now," I told her. "But it won't forever."

I saw her eyelashes flutter, and I knew she was trying to hold back tears. I couldn't change things. I knew she wouldn't go back to college. At least not for a couple of years. I knew the road wouldn't level out for a long while. As a matter of fact, it would get much rockier, much harder to traverse. She still had so much to fight against, but I couldn't do anything about that. I couldn't make it any smoother. What I could do, though, was let her know that she would survive it, no matter how bad it got.

"Look at me," I urged.

Her eyes had brightened, the green-blue of them deepened with her tears. She was so young. She was so fragile. She was so alone.

"Take a good, long look."

She didn't say anything for a long time. I knew she was seeing every wrinkle, every gray hair I'd concealed, every pound of weight I'd gained. There was so much she couldn't see. There was so much I wanted to share with her, so many things I wanted her to know, but something told me she needed to find them on her own.

"Your life will have a lot of ups and downs. For years to come, you will struggle, but you will also prevail. You'll need to remember that. Don't let go of that. You'll want to. Promise me you won't."

I stood and pulled the swing from my hips with a self-deprecating sigh. She was watching me, and I gestured her up with a wiggle of my fingers.

"Come here a minute," I said.

I gathered the younger me up into my arms, and I held her tight. I'd needed this so much back then. I'd been broken into so many pieces, sure I would never be put back together again. I felt her shake, and when she began to sob, I let her.

She cried, the sound heartbreaking to my older ears. I remembered that pain. I remembered it so well. A lifetime had happened for me between then and now, and still, I remembered it as if this wound had been inflicted just yesterday.

When she'd calmed, I held her still. I knew she wouldn't ask to be let go. I knew she wouldn't try to push away. I closed my eyes and hugged her against me.

The sound of a horn caused me to blink my eyes open. I didn't know how much time had passed. The sun was still shining above, but the coolness of the morning had burned away. The younger me had stilled in my arms, and I looked over her shoulder to see the cab that still waited for me in the parking lot. I watched as the back door opened again, telling me it was time for me to go.

I pulled away and held her face in my hands. She'd cried away the makeup she'd applied in an attempt to soften the black around her eye. The marks he'd left on her face were appalling. I knew the marks he'd left on her soul were a hundred times worse. I knew because I still carried them.

I wanted to tell her to take care of herself, but I didn't. Instead, I gave her a smile, and I left her there to climb back onto her swing and wait out the hours before she was due at work. She'd need to hide out for a little while longer. She had some decisions to make, and she'd make them no matter what I told her.

When I climbed back into the cab, Danny was waiting for me. He'd lit another cigarette and was sitting sideways so I could see his profile.

"I'm ready," I told him.

"Right on." He turned and cranked the engine.

"Hey, Danny?" I saw his eyes appear in the rearview mirror again, and I watched them for a few seconds. "Thanks."

"We're solid," he replied. "Hang onto something now," he advised. "Time to get you back to where you belong."

I took one last look out the window and saw the younger me on the swings. Her head was down again, her long hair covering the side of her face. She was fractured right now, but I knew that someday she would be whole once again.

I Know ...

I know that look
The misty one
Yes, I know it well
It comes over you in a moment
Leaves you in a haze
I know that smile
The forced one
The one I know you didn't put there
I know that clenched hand
The one around mine
The one that says you'll be back
But you don't know when
I know that hug
The one that you asked for
And the one that your numb body can't feel
I see that tear
I know about that, too
The one you cry, but you don't know why
And the one I often cry for you

1/88

The Old Switcheroo

"You want me to do what?"

He sat across the table from her and watched as the forkful of pasta she'd been lifting to her mouth stopped in mid-air.

"When was the last time you had an adventure?"

"I'm ninety-four years old. I've had my adventures. Now I want to be left alone." She ate the bite of fettuccine and chewed it while she watched him. "This is adventure enough, these Thursday night dinners with you."

Sam laughed out loud. "Italian food at Marco's Pizza is hardly what I'd call an adventure."

"That's not what the food critic for the newspaper says," Marian informed him.

"Pick someplace that cranky critic likes, and I'll take you there next week then."

"Nah. It's taken me a few years, but I've just about got the wait staff broken in. All except Harry. I'm not sure that boy can be taught. Besides, I like the breadsticks here."

Sam picked up his bottle of beer and took a long pull. He knew this wasn't going to be easy. As a matter of fact, he knew his odds of succeeding were just about nonexistent. He decided to try anyway.

"When was the last time you went on a vacation?" he asked.

"1979."

"I was only eight."

"I remember."

"That was thirty-seven years ago."

Marian dipped her chin and looked at Sam over the tops of her eye glasses. "I sure hope that expensive college education you paid so long for taught you a little something more than how to figure that out."

It took everything Sam had not to roll his eyes. Leslie had always told him he could be a real smart ass. The woman he was watching now had taught him everything he knew about the subject. "What happened in 1979?"

"Your grandad and I went to Niagara Falls to celebrate our fortieth wedding anniversary. We never made it to our fiftieth."

That part Sam knew.

"You haven't thought about traveling anywhere since?"

"Nope," Marian stated, taking a bite of her breadstick. "Nothing out there I want to see."

Sam finished off his beer. He was sure Marian was wrong about that.

...

"You might be getting senile," Marian informed him the next day. "I thought you were only forty-five. You missed our turn off. Criminy," she shook her head. "I can't take my eyes off you for even a second."

The sun was shining brightly as Sam maneuvered his SUV through the city streets.

"I know what I'm doing."

"I talked to Chloe a couple nights back. She disagrees."

Sam smiled, but it was a sad smile. "Chloe's twelve. Of course she disagrees."

"She says she's going to see you at Thanksgiving."

"That's the plan."

Marian played with the wedding ring she still wore on her finger. "That's a long time from now."

It was exactly three months. Marian was right. It was a long time.

"She starts school in a week. Leslie doesn't think it's a good idea to pull her out of class, and I agree with her."

"That's something new and different. Have you and Leslie ever agreed on anything?"

Sam pretended he hadn't heard Marian's remark. "I'll get her for a full week come November."

"California is such a long way away." Marian sighed. She looked around at the passing scenery. "I'd like to know where in the world you think you're taking me, mister."

It wasn't a question, so Sam decided to keep his mouth shut.

···

Marian was uncharacteristically quiet as Sam pulled into the short-term parking lot at the airport. She didn't utter a sound when he got out and took a suitcase and an overnight bag from the back of the car. He did receive a rather surly look when he went around and opened her door.

"You of all people ought to know better," she told him.

"You're always telling me what a bad listener I am."

"I'll say much worse to you now."

Sam couldn't help but smile. "I don't doubt that for a second."

"I don't know how you plan to get me out of this car and onto a plane of all things."

"Yeah," he shook his head. "I'm not sure how I'm gonna do that yet, either. Bribery, maybe?"

"You best start talkin'. I can't wait to find out what you come up with."

"Tell you what. How about we go inside. There's a great little shop in there. Chloe and I visit whenever she flies in. She loves their vanilla croissants. I'll buy you one and a cup of coffee or two."

Marian looked up at him, her wrinkled little face set in a stern expression. "You know you used to be my favorite."

"Used to be?"

"Hmmm," she growled as she reached for his hand. "Don't expect a Christmas present from me this year."

He raised an eyebrow. "You're coming in then?"

"For coffee and croissants," she told him. "Now help me out. All that driving around you did made me hungry."

...

Sam checked his phone again. It had been more than two hours since they'd settled into the coffee shop. He'd helped Marian to the ladies' room three times and had listened to her berate him nearly nonstop since the two of them left the car. He was starting to get worried. He knew this had been a bad idea from the start. He should never have let them talk him into this.

Marian took another sip from her coffee and brushed crumbs from the table's surface. She brought her hand up, palm facing the ceiling, and wiggled her fingers.

"What?" he asked, the strain sounding in his normally calm voice.

"Hand them over," she told him. "The tickets. Let me see them."

He reached in and pulled them from the inside pocket of his jacket. She took the envelope and gave them a thorough glance.

"Okay," she said, wrapping her scarf around her neck. "Let's get going."

Sam stared at her.

"It's been a long time since I've been to the airport, Samuel. I don't know where the gate is. Even if it's close, I think it's best we get a move on. I'm no spring chicken, you know."

She started to get up, and Sam stood to help her. He was sure she'd stall and that he'd never get her on the plane. He knew it when he'd bought the tickets, but he'd done it anyway.

He was the only boy out of five kids, and his sisters were all strong-willed women. Not one of them still lived in their hometown, and two of them were pregnant; one only a month away from her due date, the other ready to deliver at any time. When the idea of throwing a surprise party for Marian's ninety-fifth birthday popped up, it was made clear to Sam that the family couldn't come to her. She'd have to come to them. And Sam was the only one there to make that happen. The fact that Marian hadn't been interested in travelling outside the city limits in close to forty years hadn't seemed like an issue to anyone but Sam.

He decided not to overthink her acquiescence as he loaded himself up with their luggage, took Marian by the arm and headed toward the terminal.

"Don't think for a second this means I've decided to put you back on my Christmas list," she reminded him.

...

The "Fasten Seatbelts" sign flashed on, and a musical note pinged from the speakers above their heads. Seats were brought to their upright positions, and tray tables were tucked away. The flight had been uneventful. Marian even dozed for part of it, and Sam read several chapters in the new novel he'd packed into his carry on.

Once the plane landed, Marian touched Sam's arm.

"Let's wait a bit. It'll be easier for me once everyone's off. I'm not interested in being rushed or getting bumped around."

Once the cabin had quieted down, Marian reached into her purse and pulled out a strip of dark fabric. She handed it to Sam.

"What's this for?"

"It's a blindfold," she announced.

Sam raised his brow. "What on earth for?"

"It's for you."

Her answer did nothing to help him understand. "You think I can get us both off this plane with a blindfold over my eyes?"

She shook her head. "I did what you wanted me to do. Now it's your turn."

Sam bit the inside of his cheek. "This is not going to turn out well," he mused as he tied the black blindfold around his head.

"We'll see about that."

A few moments later, Sam felt someone take his arm. He allowed whomever it was to guide him out of the plane.

"I sure hope you know what you're doing," he called out to Marian.

"I always do, dear," was her response.

He sighed and continued to walk.

Soon, he felt the knot at the back of his head being loosened, and when the blindfold fell away from his eyes, he saw Chloe standing in front of him. He blinked and stared at her face.

"Hi, Dad," she said with a grin.

He looked over her head and saw the rest of his family, his four sisters in the front of the group.

"Surprise!" they all yelled, and Sam felt Marian take his arm. He looked over at her and saw a mischievous smile playing across her face.

"This is your birthday," he reminded her.

"And we both get a gift."

He smiled at her. "You sly fox. You knew all along."

She gave him a nod, then leaned into him. "I did," she told him. "Oh," she said looking up. "And about what I said earlier? Forget about it. You're still my favorite."

The Power of a Good Book
A Personal Essay
June 13, 2013

Somebody very special to me died recently. Her death should not have come as a surprise. She'd been struggling for half a dozen months, the last two of them horrendous in many ways not only for her but for her four daughters who had rallied around her and devoted their time, energy and love as they cared for her. I knew she would die soon and had known it for a while. Her mind had become a muddy, scary place due to Alzheimer's. Her sight had been leaving a little at a time in the past thirteen years since she'd be diagnosed with macular degeneration leaving her confused, unbalanced and afraid. She'd suffered two severe head injuries in the same number of months and had been left speechless and in pain by the second one. Her weight dropped and only one of her arthritic hands had the strength to grasp the fingers of her daughters or those of her grandchildren when they came to sit beside her. Her body and mind were both unsettled and agitated, rarely at peace and her legs and feet swelled beneath the bed covers.

I did not see her in this state of confusion and failing health. I am far away. More than 5,000 miles and the wide expanse of the great Atlantic Ocean have separated us for nearly two years. Three years before that there were at least seven states resting between the two of us, but that was only geography. What she and I had was history, and we had plenty of it.

There are very few memories of my childhood taking up residency in my head that do not include her in some way. For the first thirty-eight years of my life I either spoke to her on the phone or stood next to her at least three or four times a week.

I loved her when I was a small child snuggled up in bed next to her as she read books with me. I loved her as a struggling teenager, her home an undeniable refuge to me as I matured and grew into a young woman. I loved her as an adult, as a wife and then a mother of my own beautiful children who grew to know and love her as well.

There were many phone conversations these past five years. Miles and time zones stretched between us but there was always that familiarity, that bond that had begun decades earlier that had rooted itself and was neither concerned with nor diluted by distance. Letters were written, cards were sent, and visits were made. She kissed me, those light and feathery butterfly touches of her lips, and her crooked hands held tight to my fingers and I knew she loved me. I knew that as a child and now, even though she's gone, I know that still.

Another undeniable fact that I have known for some time is that someday I would lose her. The last exchange we had on the phone was memorable in ways both good and bad. The voice I heard on the other end was without a doubt the one I had known all my life. The tone and cadence lifting and falling as it always had in its soft and flowing way, but the words she spoke were nonsensical and out of context. She knew who I was but not where I was calling from. I was certainly her granddaughter, but in her mind, I had regressed somehow and was a handful of years younger than my true age. My children had become infants again and she wondered how we liked our new house although we have lived in the same place for some time. She was confused and child-like, floating along a sea of quiet chaos that her unwell mind had created, and the conversation made me sad, made me ache for the woman she had been years before.

Although I have physically not been among the other members of my family trailing in and out of the nursing home, hospital rooms and the quiet and somber halls of hospice, I have followed along through this time in the only manner I knew how from such a distance. Several times I have wondered if this absence, my not being there as her mind and body grew increasingly weak made those words I heard nearly whispered on a sob through the telephone line, "She's gone" that much harder to hear. It's impossible for me to know for sure, but even though I traveled all of those many miles back home, spoke at her funeral and watched them lower her casket into the ground, the absolute finality of her death is just now sinking in nearly three weeks after she took her last breath. The fact that I wasn't there when it happened, or even the few years before her steady decline has not made the loss of her any easier to bear, nor the pain any less severe. I lost her as much here where I am as those that spent every day with her did.

In the days that passed between her death and the long trip back to the states I understood that this would be a difficult journey. As I gathered my things and packed them up, I found myself slipping inside my bag a well-worn copy of a book I hadn't read in a while in the hopes that the story sandwiched inside the covers would take me away, even for a short time as I flew across the ocean. What I didn't remember was just how special this story is and as I read it again, first on the plane and then at night when the room I'd slept in during four years of high school was hushed and dark, the pages lit up by the buttery yellow light of the bedside lamp, I was happily reminded. I am reminded every single time I pick it up and read the text along the pages and this time I silently congratulated myself for tucking the book in with the rest of my things. It was a comfort to me, this book, and I was glad to have it with me.

To Kill a Mockingbird has been a long time favorite of countless readers. I am no different than many when I say I've read it at least a dozen different times and, although my son shakes his head at such an illogical idea, perhaps I am not the only person who believes that one can never have too many copies of one's favorite book. I have five copies of Harper Lee's masterpiece. One of them belonged to my aunt when she was in the eighth grade. Its binding is hopelessly broken, nearly a third of the pages are loose and out of order and the torn and tattered cover, which still has the price tag of sixty-nine cents stamped upon its frayed corner, is held together by a bright green rubber band. Another copy was given to me just recently by a very sweet and generous friend. It's a 35th anniversary hard cover edition in pristine condition with Harper Lee's signature marching boldly across the title page. I love each and every copy I own and will keep them all forever. Truth be told, I will probably gather a few more before it's all said and done.

My true comfort during this unhappy time came from my husband and our children; this wonderful trio that knows and has suffered from every one of my downfalls and faults a multitude of times…and loves me in spite of them all. They packed their belongings and braved the lengthy boredom of international travel to be by my side. They touched me with warm hands, held me tight, let me cry and reminisce and understood how great my loss was. I could not have gotten through it without them and am grateful to know that when a memory lights up in the corner of my mind and sadness comes to me again, they will still be there for me.

Books can't help with all that ails you, but sometimes, if you're lucky, you come across one that is so special, one that touches you in a way you simply cannot explain and, even without realizing it, you lean on its prose and strong sturdy lines of typewritten words to lend you a bit of the support you are seeking. *To Kill a Mockingbird* has done this for me. That's the power of a good book.

The Color of the Ocean

The rays of sun, so warm and bright
a shiny ribbon of gold
The water caresses the wet sand below
as the waves tell tales untold

It's about a girl who used to walk
along the sandy shore
She'd watch the seagulls fly and play
and hear the ocean's roar

Her dress would whip about her legs
Her lungs would fill with air
Taking in the lovely world
she'd made for herself there

The autumn curls bronzed by the sun
she'd pull back from her face
Intrigued by designs the seafoam made;
her ocean made of lace

She'd walk and walk upon the sand,
the beach she called her own
From sunny days to rainy nights
she'd hear the water's moan

But still the waves tell of yet one more,
a soul devoted and true
He watched the moon and the sun and the stars
and the water of green and blue

The boy would walk beside the girl
amid the salty air
The sun would shine upon his face

so beautiful and fair

She watched the wind blow at his hair
brushed back like sheaves of gold
His bright smile matched the sun's hot waves
like a fire too hot to hold

Alone they'd run in the sun all day
Two friends who'd freed their hearts
For inside each other they'd found a love
that could never tear them apart
He held her hand as they sat on the shore
and she'd count the shells at her feet
Ten for their friendship, five for the past
and one for the warm, summer heat

Each night the boy saw the green and the blue
of the ocean inside the girl's eyes
That unmistakable color he saw
in the water's afternoon tide.

She'd blink and send the waves away
and he would watch them fly
Her lashes were friends with the wind
and the ocean knew her eyes

The smile he smiled let the sun go free
and it shone bright in her eyes
It was all wrapped up there, sand and all
the wind and a seagull's cry

3/11/91

Surprise Getaway

We hadn't been dating very long. That's why I was surprised when Aaron told me he wanted to take me out of town for the weekend.

His text came at about three on Friday afternoon. He had a bag already packed, it said. He'd be at the office to pick me up at five. Don't worry about anything. All the details had already been arranged.

I went through the last two hours of work barely able to concentrate. Where was he taking me? What did this mean? Was this 'thing' we had going between us getting serious?

It had only been about six weeks ago, the night the two of us met. Truth be told, there wasn't anything about that night that hadn't been awful. It had been the night that my neighbor, Lily, was murdered in the apartment two floors above my own. A burglary gone wrong was what the police said. The newspapers reported that the assailant had been surprised to find anyone at home, that Lily lost her life because she'd decided to cancel her plans to have drinks with her friends and went to bed early instead.

Joe Tully, Lily's neighbor, was quoted in several of the articles I read. He lived in the apartment next to hers, was the one who heard her scream. He didn't even realize it had been Lily until later, until after her body had been found. He'd fallen asleep in front of the television, and when he awoke, a horror movie was on the screen. He wasn't into scary movies. He didn't know which film was playing. He said it was all dramatic music and someone had been chasing someone else. The victim in the movie was making a lot of noise. Joe never realized that the scream he'd heard, the one that had woken him up, had been real.

It was the two loud thumps he heard on the other side of the wall sometime later that got his attention. Those, he knew, had not come from the horror flick, although he'd dozed off again and didn't know how much time had passed between the two incidents.

He'd listened for a few more minutes, his head still foggy with sleep. When he heard the door close and footsteps in the hall, he jumped from his recliner. By the time he opened his own door, he was too late to save her.

He didn't have Lily's phone number. He'd thought about asking for it on several occasions, but he hadn't worked up the courage to do it yet. They were neighbors—had been for about a year— friendly but not friends. Lily was beautiful, all five feet nine of her. She worked out like a fiend, had long, dark hair, was an avid sports fan and did her own car repairs. He was sure she'd been perfect for him, Joe told me after the attack, but he'd just gotten through a nasty divorce and didn't have the nerve or the energy to jump back into the dating pool again. Now he'd lost his chance. At least with Lily.

Her door was closed but not locked. Joe called Lily's name as he walked down the foyer. He glanced around the living room. He'd never been inside Lily's apartment, so he was a poor judge as to whether things were out of place or not. It looked fine to him. He called for her again, but there was no answer.

If the door hadn't been unlocked, Joe would have second guessed the noises he'd heard. It had been a long week at work. The greasy bacon cheeseburger and large side of fries he'd washed down with three, four ... okay, five beers earlier that evening had left him not just relaxed but nearly comatose. Maybe Lily had just forgotten to lock the door before going to bed. Maybe he shouldn't be in her apartment at all. Maybe ...

Joe walked into Lily's bedroom. His huge dinner flipped in his stomach and threatened to make a second appearance. Things were not fine in here. Things were not fine at all.

Lily was on the bed, her hair fanned out around her head. It reminded Joe of every childhood drawing of the sun he'd ever seen. The strands of Lily's dark hair stretched out around her like sunbeams, but there was nothing happy or warm about the expression on her lifeless face. Her eyes were open, staring upward, but they weren't seeing anything. Nothing in this world, anyway. Her hands were spread above her head, each wrist bound to the headboard by a length of rope. Around her neck dangled a grisly necklace of torn flesh and blood, and the bra she wore had been sliced open between her breasts. She'd been beaten, no doubt violated, before her life had been taken away from her. And all while Joe had been sleeping through a horror flick on TV.

Joe called 911, but not before his dinner made good on its threat to revisit.

"Kate?"

I jumped in my chair and blinked the memories of that horrible night out of my head. When I looked up I saw Gina, a co-worker, standing next to my desk.

"Oh, hi, Gina," I said taking a deep breath of air into my lungs.

"Where were you just then? You looked a million miles away."

"I wasn't that far."

"You got a bad case of the Fridays." She grinned at me. "Fortunately for you, you only have fifteen minutes before you can hightail it on out of here. You got plans for the weekend?"

"I do, actually." I began straightening up my desk and getting ready to leave. "I'm going away with Aaron."

Gina raised an inquisitive brow. "Where to?"

I smiled. "I have no idea."

I watched as Gina grinned. "A romantic getaway weekend. Ooh, girl, you gotta love those spontaneous kinda guys," she said. "You know, Roy doesn't know the meaning of the word. It'll be pizza tonight and bowling on Sunday. It never changes." She shook her head and reached down to nudge my arm. "You'll be sure to tell me all about it come Monday, right? I'll live vicariously."

"Well," I laughed. "Let's just wait and see if there's anything interesting to tell first, shall we?"

...

Aaron was waiting for me just like he said he would be, sitting out in front of my building in his black Mercedes. When I slid into the passenger's seat he gave me a smile.

"Ready to go?" he asked, leaning forward to press a kiss against my cheek. "I have a fun weekend planned for us."

I returned his smile when he pulled away. "Okay, let's go."

He pulled the car into traffic, and I studied his profile, thinking about the first time I saw him.

Much of the apartment complex had been alerted by the sounds of sirens once Joe called the police. The ambulance arrived, and soon afterward, officers were going door to door questioning tenants about anything they might have seen or heard to aid them in their search for the murderer.

I stood in the hallway in front of Joe's door, my body wrapped in a terry cloth robe, my feet in socks that slouched around my ankles. It was nearly two in the morning and, although I'd only known Joe for about half an hour, I was doing my best to console him.

The police gathered a few people that were wandering the hall near Lily's door and brought them into Joe's apartment. I couldn't help but hear one of the officer's as he questioned a man dressed in pajama pants and a white t-shirt. Joe rented a one bedroom, and the space had filled up fast.

"Do you live on this floor, sir?"

"No," the pajama clad man said with a shake of his disheveled head. "I mean, yes, I'm staying in an apartment on this floor, but I don't live here. I'm dog sitting for a friend who's out of town."

"Which apartment?"

"404."

"That's what, two doors down?"

"Yes, sir."

"Did you know Lily Andrews?"

He shook his head. "Except for my friend, I don't know anyone in the building."

"Did you hear anything? Any strange sounds? Anything at all out of the ordinary?"

"I was listening to music," the man explained, reaching up to brush the hair away from his eyes. "I'd fallen asleep with my headphones on. I'm afraid I didn't hear anything. I'm sorry."
"How long are you dog sitting for your friend?"

"She comes back this afternoon."

The officer gave him a dip of his chin and moved on to another tenant who had been pulled into the small living room. I turned to check on Joe, but he was sitting on the edge of his couch, a paramedic talking him through some deep breathing exercises. His face was white, and his hairline was wet with sweat. He wasn't looking so good. I feared he'd either hyperventilate or pass out.

"This is crazy." I turned at the voice and realized white t-shirt guy was still standing there. "Just awful."

I nodded in agreement. I was in shock and found it difficult to come up with a response.

He moved forward, placed a warm hand on my arm. "Are you okay?"

"No," I finally said. "No, I'm not. Not really."

"Maybe you should get out of here." He tilted his head in Joe's direction. "Looks like your friend is in good hands. It would probably do you good to be back in your own place." I watched him without speaking. The circumstances seemed unreal. I couldn't wrap my head around it all. "Come on," he urged, guiding me by the elbow. "Tell me where you live. I'll make sure you get there safely."

"Second floor," I mumbled. "Apartment 200."

We stepped into the elevator. When the doors closed, most of the sound went away. "I'm Aaron Murray," he told me. "And you are?"

I looked up at him. "Kate. Kate Miller." The elevator stopped. I didn't move when the doors parted, and Aaron took my elbow again. He led me down the hall and toward my apartment, pulling the keys from my hand.

"Do you have your phone with you?"

"My phone?"

He smiled. "Let me see it a minute."

I reached in and fished my phone out of the pocket of my robe. We exchanged the phone and keys and I watched him tap on the screen without a thought about what he was doing. When he handed it back, I felt him gently push me inside my home.

"I saved my number for you. Call me in a few days, let me know how you're doing."

"Oh," I said. "Okay."

"I'm going to shut the door now. Make sure you lock it. I won't leave until I hear the bolt click."

He disappeared, and I leaned my head against the wood.

"Kate?" he said after a while.

I swallowed back tears and reached up to engage the lock.

"Try to get some sleep."

I didn't answer. Instead, I walked to my bedroom, climbed into bed and pulled the covers over my head.

...

I did call him. I didn't mean to. Well, I did, but only because I couldn't remember who Aaron Murray was, or why I had his number in my contact list.

He remembered right away who I was.

"Kate," he said when he answered the phone.

"Um, hi," I replied, trying to place his voice.

"I'm glad you called. It's been a couple weeks. Hear anything more about your neighbor?"

My neighbor. Lily. Aaron Murray. White t-shirt guy.

I took a deep breath. "No," I said, shaking my head even though he couldn't see it. "No, they still don't know who killed her."

"Listen," he said. "I have an idea."

"What's that?"

"How about we go out for coffee and come up with something more pleasant to talk about?"

As the weeks went by, coffee turned to drinks. Then it turned to dinner, and now it had turned into a weekend away. I watched as Aaron smiled. I'd been staring as I recalled the unusual start to our relationship. He glanced over and moved his hand to my thigh. He gave it a squeeze and I smiled back.

"Where are we going?" I asked.

"You'll see soon enough."

My smile grew wider. "What will we do when we get there?"
"I've got something fun planned," he answered mysteriously.

It was clear I would get nothing more from him, so I sat back in my seat, relaxed, and enjoyed the scenery.

...

The suitcase he'd packed for me sat on the bed. I saw it as soon as I walked out of the bathroom. My face was flushed from the cocktails I'd drunk at dinner, and I wasn't feeling very steady on my feet. I was euphoric, the feeling helped by the alcohol but fueled by an enjoyable night out.

"Go ahead," Aaron told me, motioning toward the suitcase. "There's something in there you might like to try on."

I grinned. Perhaps the evening was going to get even better.

The zipper was smooth as I pulled it down one side and across the front. It wasn't a large suitcase, and not one I'd seen before. No one had ever packed a bag for me or whisked me off on a weekend adventure. I laughed quietly when I thought about the story I'd have to share with Gina come Monday.

I flipped the top back and scanned the contents of the case. On top lay a bra and panty set. They were made of satin and black lace, and the heat in my cheeks intensified. I picked the panties up and saw a large envelope beneath them with my name scrawled across the front.

"What's this?" I asked.

"Why don't you look and find out?"

I lifted the envelope and tugged the flap open. I reached in and pulled out a sheaf of papers. No, not papers, photographs. I turned them so the photo on the top of the stack was right side up. When I realized what I was looking at, my breath caught in my chest.

It was a woman. She was about my age and lying on a bed. She had long, dark hair and there was blood. Lots and lots of blood.

It was Lily.

"What?" I asked, dropping the photos. They fell into the suitcase, and I could see that there were several more just like the one on top. I scattered them with my hands. Women. All of them different. All of them dead. All of them wearing black bras and panties. Their throats all gaping in a fatal, red smile.

My vision blurred for a moment, and I moved the photos again, my fingers brushing against something rough. I dug in, wrapped my hand around it and pulled it out. It was a coil of rope.

"Aaron?" I looked up to see that he'd moved closer. He was staring down at me with a cold, hard smile.

He pulled a knife from behind his back. The blade glinted in the light from the bedside table. "I told you I had something fun planned."

Small-Town Girl

Eve was curled up in her seat, pretending to be asleep. She'd trailed after her mom through the jet bridge, barely keeping up while harried passengers bumped and prodded her along. Once they'd boarded the plane and found their seats, her mom urged her into the row first, gushing about how fortunate it was that they'd been able to get a window seat even though she'd made reservations just a week before.

"The plane is full," she said. "I'll bet there isn't even a single empty seat and yet here we are." She balanced a bouquet of flowers their neighbors had brought over to the house before they'd left for the airport in on arm while trying to stow her carry on into the already overflowing bin above her head. "Go on," she said, gently prodding her sluggish daughter toward the window. "It's a clear morning. You ought to be able to see plenty before the plane gains altitude."

Caroline Reilly really was a wonder. There were times when Eve wished she could muster up even a small portion of the excitement her mom seemed to feel about any number of different things. She wasn't sure if all the enthusiasm that poured forth from Caroline in the form of smiles and overwhelming positivity was genuine, but she had to admire the effort the woman exerted. Although it was oftentimes annoying as hell—in this instance especially—Eve had to admit, her mom's optimistic tenacity was impressive.

The longer Eve was stuck on the plane, and the further the giant bird flew east, the more uneasy she became. It was as if her home town and her heart were physically and emotionally connected. She felt the strain grow more painful with each mile that separated them.

She'd played with magnets before. She'd always marveled at how the stronger ones pulled from her fingers to snap together even when she held them apart. West Linn was a magnet. So was her heart, and the two of them were straining mightily to reconnect.

The house she'd grown up in, the one in West Linn, was a part of her. It had been for the last fourteen years. Although it was only a thirty-minute drive from Portland, West Linn had always seemed like its own little world. She'd been surrounded by hills, trees and rivers. There was the big Willamette River, and then Tanner Creek, which ran along the lower border of the Reilly property. That's where she'd gone when she needed some time to think. It was so quiet, so isolated down there. The trees soared high, and when she looked straight up, she could see a wide expanse of dark, black sky. She'd even seen a shooting star once or twice.

She'd thought about a lot of things over the years down there on the old bridge that stood above the cold, clear water of Tanner Creek. How was she going to hide that D she'd gotten in art class? Art class of all things. Was it her fault she wasn't artistically inclined? And what about Micah? Was he going to ask her to the homecoming dance, or would she be stuck going with Amber and Laura?

The question she'd pondered the most in the last couple of weeks while her feet hung over the worn, wooden planks of Tanner Bridge was how in the world was she, a small-town girl, ever going to survive in Manhattan of all places? How would she ever see the stars in the sky through the glow of lights in the city that never sleeps?

"It won't be that bad," Caroline told her, bringing Eve out of her own thoughts for a moment.

Eve could barely hear her mother's voice with the ear buds she had stuffed in her ears. That was another annoying thing about her mom. It was almost as if she could read Eve's thoughts sometimes. She thought about responding but couldn't think of a single thing to say. It was easier to pretend she hadn't heard, that she was asleep, even though it was obvious her mother knew better.

Any conversation Eve and Caroline had now would be no different than the ones they'd had over the past week anyway. Eve wasn't interested in being told even one more time just how blessed they were that her father had gotten this new job. People were out of work all over the country, and her father had been fortunate for a long time. He'd survived years of cut backs and layoffs and had never been out of work. It was a wonder he'd gone this long the way things were going.

Even if she hadn't been told a hundred times or more, Eve knew all these things were true. She was only fourteen, but she was a smart girl. She paid attention. And there probably wasn't a single person on this planet she loved more than Craig Reilly. She was a daddy's girl. She always had been. Although she wasn't yet old enough to fully comprehend the situation from her father's point of view, she understood well enough just how frightened her father was at the thought of not being able to support his family.

"It's hard to find a good, high paying job," he'd told Eve one night at the dinner table. "I've applied to at least fifty of them so far, but it's like shooting craps." His smile had been almost apologetic as he leaned closer to her. "You know how much I suck at gambling, right? I lose every time, but today I finally managed to get a good roll of the dice."

He explained that he'd been contacted by a company who liked what they saw in his resumé. He'd done an interview over the phone, then was told they wanted to see him in person for a more formal meeting.

That had been two weeks ago. Five days after the interview, he'd called and told Caroline he'd received a job offer.

"The clouds are clearing," Caroline told Eve that afternoon when she'd come home from school, her eyes bright with happiness. Eve had to admit, it had felt unusually stormy in the Reilly household for some time. The big lightning bolt of sudden unemployment had hit the family hard, and Caroline was sure that this new job was the colorful rainbow they'd sought, powerful enough to chase away the heavy rain clouds.

Eve was less convinced. Even if she was apt to find sweetness and light in even the darkest of circumstances like her mother was known to do, Eve knew what she'd discover at the end of this particular rainbow would be a high-rise apartment building instead of a shiny pot of gold.

The flight was a long one, and Eve felt cramped as she heard the overhead ding warning passengers that their seatbelts should now be fastened. She glanced up and saw that her mother held a book in her lap, a finger indicating her place in the text, but it lay unopened. The bouquet of flowers had been stuffed in the pocket in front of her mother's seat. They weren't looking so good, and the fabric below the wilted blooms was still a bit damp from the small, leaking vial that had once held water.

Eve blinked and tried to stretch her legs as best she could, catching Caroline's smile as her mother turned her head.

"I did some research," Caroline said. Eve reached up and wrapped her fingers around the wires hanging from her neck and pulled the ear buds out of her ears. "I know you're going to miss Tanner Bridge, but we won't be all that far from Central Park. There are several bridges there you might grow to like just as much."

Eve opened her mouth to tell her mom that none of them would be the same, but Caroline shook her head and hurried her own words.

"There are eleven of them," Caroline went on. "And twenty-two arches." She shrugged her shoulders. "I've never seen them, but I suppose they might count."

"Mom—"

"There's the Gothic Bridge," Caroline continued, undeterred. "It stands between the reservoir and the tennis courts. Then there's the Gapstow Bridge. It crosses The Pond." She tipped her chin down and watched her daughter. "That's capitalized, by the way. The Pond." She enunciated the words. "That bridge stands twelve feet high and was built in 1896."

"That's pretty old." Eve felt the plane as it began to descend. Her stomach gave a little lurch, and she turned her head to catch her first glimpse of New York City out of the small, rectangular window she'd been leaning against for most of the flight.

"The bridge I most want to see is the Bow Bridge. Remember watching that movie with me? You know, the one with Jenna Elfman and the guy who plays the Hulk?"

"Mark Ruffalo?" Eve hadn't looked back over at Caroline. Her eyes were still staring out the window as the plane slowly fell from the sky.

"No, no," Caroline said with a shake of her head. "The first guy. Well," she amended. "Not the first. I'm not talking about the bodybuilder." She was quiet for a few seconds. "Edward!" she exclaimed when she remembered. "Edward Norton."

"Oh," Eve said. "Yeah. Him."

"Well, the Bow Bridge. It was in that movie. Edward Norton plays a priest. It was very funny. We'll have to watch it again, and then we can visit the bridge. I read it's the largest one in the whole park. It'll be fun to walk across it after seeing it in a film, don't you think?"

They were nearly on the ground, and Eve scrunched her eyes shut. She'd always hated this part. Landing was the worst. She realized then that her mom must have remembered and was trying to distract her.

"Yeah, Mom," she said, a bit of gratefulness seeping into the fear and sadness that crowded her chest. "You're right. That will be cool." She trapped the breath in her lungs and held it there. She felt Caroline's hand cover her own just seconds before the wheels of the plane touched down on the runway. She braced herself as the pilot hit the brakes and kept her eyes closed tight.

It was official. The Reilly's had become New Yorkers. In her heart, though, Eve knew she'd probably always be a small-town girl.

Backyard Fairyland
A Personal Essay
August 20, 2016

I have some of the most amazing memories of my dad's backyard. When I think about it now, I wonder if it was actually as great as I remember it, or if I'm just recalling it from an imaginative child-like state of mind. I haven't been in his backyard for more than twenty years. I'm not even sure if his widow still owns the property—but I think I'd rather not see it as it is now. My memories of it are profound and beautiful, and I'd like them to stay that way.

As I sit and write this, I am well aware of the fact that I used that backyard as a sanctuary; a safe place from what went on inside the house. Maybe that makes my memories of that space even more special. I also think that things were different when I was a child. I spent a lot of time outside, regardless of where I was. There was no internet or high-tech video games to keep me inside. There was exploring and bike riding, roller skating on uneven pavement and playing. Just playing. I had some incredible adventures in that backyard.

There are so many things I remember about that magical space—and yes, it was magical in so many ways.

There was a huge apple tree that shot up into the blueness of the sky, its branches stretching out to canopy a large part of the thick, green grass below. The apples the tree bore were never very large. They were hard and round as golf balls, but I remember picking the ones I could reach, or catching them as my dad shook the taller boughs.

I'd fill my arms with them and sit in the shade of that tree trying to chase away the sharp, sour flavor of the bright, green fruit with a salt shaker. Did they taste particularly good? Not really. They made me pucker my mouth, and they tightened the back of my jaw, but it didn't matter. I still eagerly anticipated them every year.

I don't know just how big in acreage the yard was. I do know that it seemed big to me as a kid. There was a collection of trees, all with thin trunks and long, skinny branches that made up a straight-lined border between my dad's property and the one next to it. His neighbors, the Miller's, were an elderly couple. They were incredibly friendly and encouraged me to wander through those trees. They had a cement donkey sitting in their front yard. It stood less than two feet high, and was, even then, a pretty small statue, but it didn't stop me from sitting on it, wild adventures playing through my young, blonde head.

I would visit the Millers' backyard when I'd hear them outside. Mrs. Miller was blind. I remember sitting outside with her and chattering like a little bird. She would ask me all kinds of questions, and I would eagerly answer them. We would sometimes end up in their kitchen, which was at the back of their house, and she would feed me cookies or cake while we sat at her table.

On the other side of my dad's property was an old, black wire fence. I used to sit on it and bounce. I was never told not to, and I was small back then, so I doubt I did much damage to it. The yard on the other side of that fence was amazing, too. It belonged to a family both my mom and dad had known since they were young. Their last name was Willie.

There were paths with white wooden archways built over them, and lots and lots of rose bushes in that yard. I would walk the short distance down Bradburn Boulevard to the black gate in front of Mrs. Willie's yard.

I would wander through her gardens and smell all the colorful flowers I found there. She was elderly as well, but we were always welcome to visit. I remember being inside her house many times, but it was in her garden I felt most comfortable.

At the far end of my dad's yard, past the lawn and the towering apple tree, was a grape vine. It was unruly and unkempt, growing along an aging trellis, the leaves huge and twisting every which way. My dad was Greek. I remember going to a Greek festival once with him and my grandmother. We ate dolmades—stuffed grape leaves—at the festival. Granny always talked about making some of her own every time she was out in the yard, but if she did make them, I don't recall it. I do remember picking some of the grapes and eating them. Every edible thing that came out of that yard was sour—the apples, the grapes, and the cherries that grew on the half dozen trees that stood inside the grape vine arch—but I ate them anyway. Probably just because I could.

There was a ditch that ran along Bradburn Boulevard, right in front of my dad's house. During the summer, the city allowed the homeowners to temporarily dam the ditch and use the water to irrigate their lawns. It only happened once or twice a summer, but I remember those days fondly. My dad would nearly flood the back yard, and I would put my swimming suit on and use the wide expanse of wet, soggy grass as a humongous Slip 'n Slide. The water was always icy cold, and I had mud and bits of grass stuck to my arms and legs, but it was so much fun.

I also remember playing in the sheets that my mom, and then later, my step-mom, hung on the laundry lines that ran down part of the length of that yard. I would play with the clothes pins that were dropped in the grass and play hide and seek with the cats that called my dad's place home. When I got tall enough, I would jump and grab the thick, metal T at the top of the pole, and I would swing from the bar.

I have often said that one day I would write a book about this yard. As I write this post, I realize that I already have—or at least this yard inspired one quite a bit like it. It is the yard I wrote about in The Color of Thunder, although that one was in a different part of the country, and in a much different climate. The way the Linsey children in that book felt about their yard is much the same way I felt about my father's.

This backyard was like a fairyland; a wonderful memory, and a place I am so grateful I was able to call my own for a great number of years.

Flawed

This feeling was nothing new. This feeling that she was a failure—that everything she touched was tinged with the discolored stain of "it could've been done better". It was never easy, these chunks of time. Fortunately, she wasn't plagued by them often, but this one really had a hold of her. It seemed to be just a little bit harder to bear than some of the others had been.

She stood in the shower letting the hot water pound against the backs of her shoulders. Hard water. It clogged the shower head and made the stream unpredictable at best. The nozzle was turned to the pulse setting—not because an overly hard massage was what she was after, but because it was the only way the pipes could push out enough water to make a shower worthwhile.

She turned slightly, a jet of water finding its way through one of the only holes not calcified shut. It was just one stream, but, it habitually found the most tender spot on her body, and for some reason, she was surprised by it.

Sleep had been elusive and filled with thoughts that caused her chest to tighten. There was so much going on in her head. How could she possibly be expected to remember that one goddamn jet?

Her mind was busy. It always was, but lately it had been even more so. It sped and spun at a breathtaking rate, the gears never slowing. She was known as the talkative sort. Chatty. Maybe even too much sometimes—but the funny thing about that was, there was still so much she never said. She didn't share a lot of the big stuff. At least not very often. Her tribe, as it were, was an incredibly small one.

She was afraid, and oftentimes the fear manifested itself in tears. This made her look weak, which was far from the truth. She was sentimental, though, and highly emotional. Sensitive, too, damn it all. Maybe that's why she was so afraid.

There was reason to be. She'd dropped the ball. She shook her head and uttered a humorless laugh. It echoed in the shower stall and vibrated around her. She'd failed. It had been happening a lot lately.

That nagging feeling was back. It visited from time to time like that unwanted guest who seemed to show up at the least convenient time. You know, those times when there is a multitude of things to get done and the guest bathroom hasn't been cleaned in a month? He wears out his welcome the second he steps over the threshold, but he continues to stay, demanding hospitality from a host who can't seem to scrounge up any. It consumed her. She was distracted and exhausted by it. And he was a cheeky devil. She wasn't the violent type, but she wanted to kick this soul sucking guest right in his devious face.

The feeling taunted her. "I'm not surprised. You fucked up again, just like I knew you would. And this time you did it up good, didn't you?"

"Damn it!" She had. She knew it, and she hated herself for it.

She reached up and slammed the handles of the faucet up. The inconsistent stream of water ceased, and the only other sound in the small room was the dripping in the drain below her feet. The metal felt smooth beneath her unmanicured toes. It was probably the hard scrubbing she'd given it the day before. She sucked at that, too. The house was never put together enough. It felt like she was always picking stuff up or cleaning something, but it had gotten out of control. It always did.

Without thinking about it, she sighed. There was a cloud of steam in the room—a crazy space that, in most likelihood, was never meant to be a bathroom. She'd never seen the blueprints for the original structure she lived in but surmised at one time this had been a walk-in closet. The doorway was much too narrow, and it didn't have a door. Master bathroom my ass, she thought.

Although the house was a year older than she was, it had only been owned by two other families. She didn't know exactly how they'd changed the house, but she knew it had been altered. Outside, it looked stately, dressed up in blond colored brick with a curved entry. Visitors complimented it all the time. Pizza delivery people, parents escorting their candy crazed children at Halloween ... even the uniformed employees who came to the door trying to sell her overpriced cable packages told her how gorgeous, how remarkable the house was. She supposed on the outside it wasn't too bad. It wasn't the prettiest house on the block, but it held its own.

The inside was a whole different story. It was nonsensical and uneven. Nothing matched from room to room, and there were telltale strips of paint in various shades around the windowsills that hinted at all the different styles and colors it had worn throughout the years. The doors were broken. Sometimes they stuck, and she had to throw her hip against the wood to get them to open. Other times they wouldn't latch correctly or stay closed. The floors were mismatched, the hardwoods old and worn out, and the smelly, stained carpet had been pulled up and discarded long ago.

The house had been her doing. There hadn't been much of a choice, really. There were only two places on the short list. The budget was tight, and it had been up to her alone. She probably should have picked the other house. It was a lot smaller, but it was also a lot newer with fewer ragged edges and badly concealed blemishes. The yard had been finished, it was in a better neighborhood, and the wall behind the built-in entertainment cabinet had been a magical shade of deep turquoise. Space would have been a problem, but ...

The air was cool to her heated skin as she stepped out of the shower. The other house—she couldn't even remember the name of the street it had been on, which was unusual because she remembered damn near everything—had been appealing. It hadn't spoken to her, though, except to say that she'd never fit the dining room table they'd just purchased into that tiny little kitchen, and what about office space?

This house—the one with the bricked in fireplace that took up an entire wall in the basement, the one that had the bathroom with the blue mermaid tiles on the floor downstairs and a red sink in the kitchen—had spoken to her. She thought she'd grasped the message at the time and was almost certain it had been a good one. Looking back on it now, though, she realized that it was entirely possible that she might have misunderstood it. As time went on, she became more and more convinced that the line of communication she thought she'd shared with the house years ago had been plagued by a fuzzy connection, and she'd missed something important, something vital that she should have caught before she made the fateful decision to move her family within its four walls. The scariest part of the whole thing was she was beginning to think both she and the house had a lot in common. They both meant well, and they tried really hard. On the exterior, they looked like they had their shit together, but inside they were both disorganized, perhaps a little broken and extraordinarily messy.

Oh, and then there was that visitor that kept coming to call. He'd conveniently ignored the fact that neither she nor the house had a welcome mat outside their front doors. He wasn't big on manners, and had, on countless occasions, rudely walked right on in without so much as knocking first.

She dressed in her bedroom—the one that still had more than half the old wallpaper on the walls. It was some Oriental theme. At least she thought it was. It was dirty white with pale blue, and all four walls had a different design.

The one she stared at while pulling her jeans on had a ragged edge that ran halfway down the right side and she could see the glue underneath; old, yellow and ugly.

Things were really screwed up. They weren't working right. It felt monumental, overwhelming, like there was too much to deal with. There had been so many bad decisions made—both having to do with her personal life and the design of the house— and with each one, the debt grew larger. It was time to pay up, and the price was incredibly high.

Could it be fixed? She wasn't sure. She stood at the end of the long hall, her eyes catching sight of the four doors that lined both sides. Every one of them was different, and the floor she stood on felt slightly bumpy beneath her feet. She took a deep breath and steeled herself for the day. With time and renovation, she hoped that maybe both of them could be saved.

Season

Quiet, padded footsteps heard in the narrow hall
Behind her lies a closed door,
before her waits a door unbolted
Closer and closer she walks
so safe and guarded
fixed between
She gingerly fingers the golden knob,
releasing the clasp with her touch
Peering inside
to wonder
to look
The shiny foil colors
of the winged butterflies
reflect in her turquoise eyes ...
The warm breeze kisses her skin
and her golden hair blows back away from her shoulders
baring the heart encased within.

10/16/89

The Monster Under My Bed
A True Story … Mostly

Something brought me up from a deep sleep. A noise of some sort. Not loud, just pronounced enough to catch my attention.

I lie still, my body relaxed and tired.

Then the noise came again. Scuffling.

I wasn't afraid. I knew exactly what the source of the disturbance was. Be still, I told myself, silently. Maybe he'll go back to sleep.

My bed was warm, and the day had been long. I wasn't sure how many hours I'd slept, but I knew I needed a few more before I was ready to face the day ahead.

I'd just managed to doze off again when I felt an abrupt shove from beneath, and I was bounced off my mattress. My eyes popped open, and a sound of surprise escaped my throat. There would be no going back to sleep now.

"Sorry."

The voice came from under the bed. It was deep and rumbly. And incredibly sad.

"What's up, big guy?" I asked.

I heard a sigh and more movement beneath the box springs.

"Neither one of us will rest until you tell me what's wrong. Come on," I urged.

It took him a few moments to climb from his spot, but once he was out, he was surprisingly light on his sized fourteen feet. He stood, rectangular-shaped head drooping from a neck that sported silver bolts on each side.

I reached over and patted the bed. I'd known him for a long time. More than forty years, in fact, and I could tell when he had something on his mind. "Sit."

He did as I asked, and the mattress bowed beneath his weight. It was hard to see him in the dark. I knew he wore black pants, the cuffs of which didn't quite reach the tops of his boots. His jacket was also black, the sleeves sitting high upon his long forearms, and his shirt, once white, had been in serious need of a washing for some time. I'd offered on several occasions, but he was reluctant to part with it. It was hard to figure a monster out sometimes.

"Mind if I turn the light on?" I asked.

"Nope."

I reached over and clicked on the bedside lamp. The room was filled with a buttery yellow light, and I fluffed up my pillows before resting against them. "Was I being restless?"

He looked up at me, his black hair mussed and a trickle of blood that never dried coloring his left temple. He gave me a nod.

"Mark," he said.

The sound of the name startled me. "Where did you find that?" I exclaimed.

"In here," he answered, reaching over to tap the top of my head with his long index finger. "I tried to keep it away."

"You did," I assured him. "Thank you."

"That one is stubborn."

I sighed, feeling badly that he'd had another tussle with a memory that should have given up and vacated its space in my head years ago.

I studied my monster's face. I didn't much like calling him a monster, but he and I had been over that time and time again. He'd made it clear back when I was young that this was one argument I wasn't likely to win.

The two of us met when I was five. I'd been in California, on a trip with my family at the time. I'd always been a timid little girl, one who was easily frightened. We were in line, waiting to buy admission tickets for Universal Studios. The Jaws ride had just debuted that year, and, although I was young, I remember people being excited about it.

My dad was carrying me. That in itself is an uncomfortable recollection. I don't have many memories of an affectionate nature when it comes to my father. I saw the monster from across the way. He was mingling with those who were waiting to purchase tickets, trying, I suppose, to help them pass the time. He's a very large monster, and easy to spot.

He turned and caught my wide-eyed gaze, and suddenly, I was staring up into a green face, put together much like a patchwork quilt with dark, stitched lines of blood and a strange mop of black hair stuck on top of his irregularly shaped head. My five-year-old self went into panic mode, and I nearly climbed myself right out of my father's arms.

There was an exchange of words between my dad and the monster, the latter curious about what they called me and how old I was. I remember my dad telling him my name was Jennifer. When the monster spoke to me, however, that's not the name he used.

"Hello, Jenny," the monster rumbled in a deep and quiet voice. "Don't be afraid."

It was way too late for that. I'd hit afraid and run full throttle to terrified by that point. He continued to talk to me, but I refused to turn and look at him again. I was sobbing and well beyond consolation.

The monster haunted me for years after that. Literally, for since that day, he's been with me. As a child, I would lie in my bed, straight as a board, afraid that he would grab a wayward limb should I be careless enough to let one dangle over the mattress. I knew he was there, camped out beneath me. I could hear him breathing. If I had to use the bathroom in the middle of the night, I would take a flying leap from my bed and land with a thump several feet toward the center of my room so that he couldn't reach out and grab one of my ankles. The return trip was a little more difficult, but at least my bladder wasn't full. He never got me. Not once.

On several occasions, I'd gather up enough courage to peek over the edge of my bed. Sometimes I couldn't see him. Other times he'd be lying there in the space between the wall and the bedframe. Like I said, his size is noteworthy, and he didn't fit beneath my twin bed all that well. He would look up at me, but he didn't speak. In my young, child-sized heart, I just knew this beast meant to do me harm, and the thought of him frightened me for years.

That is until one night when a particularly nasty nightmare came to visit.

Fear overwhelmed me. I cried, and tears streamed down my face to plaster long strands of hair to my cheeks. My heart was racing, and I thrashed beneath the covers. My nightmares were so vivid that night that I was without doubt that they were real. I don't recall any of them now. What I will never forget, however, is what chased those shadowy demons away.

The monster under my bed.

You may know him as Frankenstein. That's not entirely accurate. Anyone who's read Mary Shelley's book will tell you that he's not Frankenstein, but Frankenstein's monster. That name is not one he's terribly fond of, though. Early on in our relationship he asked me to call him Eli. I think it suits him quite nicely. Besides, he's my monster now.

It took me a long time to realize, years in fact, that Eli wasn't there to scare me, and he certainly wasn't there to do me harm. Quite the opposite, really. He was there to keep the bad stuff away, kind of like a dreamcatcher—if dreamcatchers were almost seven feet tall and grumbly with green skin and bolts keeping their heads attached to their bodies. It was his job to filter out as much of the scary, as much of the unpleasant as he could, and to soothe me when any of it got past him.

He explained to me that almost everyone has a monster that lives under their bed. Those who don't just haven't come across the right monster yet. That day in California, that day Eli spotted me waiting in line at Universal Studios, that was the day he knew he'd found his person. He'd meant what he'd said. He didn't want me to be afraid.

I reached out and touched his arm. Eli blinked at me and gave me a closed-mouth smile.

"Feel better now?" I asked.

He nodded his large head. "I do." I reached up and wrapped my arms around his broad and uneven shoulders. I felt him pat me on the back with one of his large hands.

"Thanks for keeping me safe, Eli," I told him.

I heard him sniff. He's always been the sentimental kind.

He pulled away from my hug and gave me a wink as he climbed back to the dark den below my box springs. Just like on many other occasions, I thought to offer him the couch before I stopped myself. He'd just tell me no. After all, where do monsters belong if not under the bed?

The Nutcracker and the Cheeseball
A Modern (and Humorous) Take
on E.T.A. Hoffmann's Classic Fairy Tale
The Nutcracker and the Mouse King

The story begins on Christmas Eve at the Wing house …

J.C. sits in her living room speculating about what kind of present her godfather, Drosselmeyer, a very talented clockmaker and inventor, has made for her. The guy is a little off, and she's believed this the entire time she's known him. Still, he gives great gifts, and he has a wicked sense of humor. Humor, in J.C.'s opinion, is a very important thing.

The wait is long, and she almost falls asleep. Christmas is a busy time of year, and J.C. is a bit worn out.

At last Drosselmeyer arrives. She perks up when she is presented with his gift, which turns out to be a nutcracker. She has no idea why he decided to make such a thing … but the doll intrigues her with his unusual face and his jacket the color of candied cherries. Even more than that, though, she is thrilled with the fact that he will provide her with a snack. She has been so busy wrapping those last-minute presents and baking cookies for the families that live in her cul-de-sac that she forgot to eat a proper dinner.

Her stomach growls in protest. She finds a bag of mixed nuts—where did those come from?—and begins to put Drosselmeyer's gift to good use. Unfortunately, she tries to crack one that is too hard, and the nutcracker's jaw breaks.

After some very colorful (and quiet—it is Christmas Eve, after all) swearing, J.C. heaves a frustrated sigh and pulls an old ACE bandage from the depths of her bag. It's bedraggled and hasn't been rolled up properly, but it will have to do.

She carefully wraps it around the wounded nutcracker, keeping his lower jaw snug against the top, lining up the painted white teeth. She shakes her head sadly as she pats his shiny, wooden hat. So much for snack time.

When everyone has left the living room and it's finally time for bed, J.C. knows she should probably do a quick clean up. She looks around the space, her mood on this side of defeated. She is so exhausted. The house is always a little messy. Okay, maybe even a tad more than a little. She has several talents, but housekeeping has never been one of them.

She looks around and spots the nutcracker. Feeling a bit guilty for breaking him, she reaches out and runs her fingers over his soft, feathery beard. She tells him in a quiet voice that she will ask Drosselmeyer to fix his jaw, hoping the old man will be able to find some time in his busy life as a retiree to make the repairs. Honestly, she is surprised he opted for homemade gifts this year instead of doing his shopping online. She knows he's on a bowling league, and she overheard him talking earlier in the evening about the trips he was making to the coast. He'd tried surfing not long ago and found it rather entertaining. It seems odd that he would spend so much time on strange little gifts such as this wooden soldier, but to each his own.

J.C. studies the nutcracker before giving him a smile and a shrug. He is strange, but handsome—in an odd and unexplainable way. As she tells the nutcracker this, his face seems to come alive momentarily. J.C. blinks, surprised. Then she shrugs it off.

What's crazier? The fact that she thought she saw a wooden soldier smile at her, or that she was talking to one in the first place? Perhaps she has imbibed in one too many glasses of wine, she reasons, lying back against the couch.

The grandfather clock begins to chime. Wait. She doesn't have a grandfather clock. Still, as J.C. stares across the room, she is almost sure she sees one there—and that Drosselmeyer is perched precariously on top of it, refusing to let it strike. Okay, maybe she has had too many glasses of wine.

She hears a scratching noise. It's coming from below the ground. It starts out soft, then gets louder, and soon, J.C. sees mice begin to emerge from beneath the floor boards. She'd been meaning to get the hardwoods redone, but she had no idea they were in this state. When she spies a seven-headed Mouse King rise from the honey-stained slats, she shakes her head in disbelief.

Wow. It was true what they said. The holidays really could bring about some serious stress.

A sudden movement to J.C.'s right makes her jump. She turns to see a dozen dolls stored in a toy cabinet come to life. Toy cabinet? J.C. shakes her head. That must have come from the same place the nuts and the clock did. The dolls? She thought those had all been stored away years ago, but here they were—and they seemed to be taking direction from the nutcracker, who was forcefully taking command and leading them into battle with the mice. The wooden soldier held the old ACE bandage in one hand and turned his body so that his painted eyes could focus on J.C. "A token" he says in a strange, deep voice, then he forged ahead to take on the army of rodents.

He and the dolls seem to be winning, at least at first, but soon they are overwhelmed by the mice. J.C. watches as the nutcracker is trapped. He is about to be taken prisoner. For reasons she can't explain, J.C. feels as though she needs to save him. She takes off her New Balance sneaker and aims it at the Mouse King's head. Or one of them, anyway. The sudden movement makes her alcohol-soaked brain swim, and she loses her balance. She isn't sure if she's hit the large rodent because a sharp, stinging pain diverts her attention. She's put her arm clean through the glass of the toy cabinet, cutting it badly. The last thing she sees before she faints and falls back to the couch is deep, red blood dripping from the wound. Oh, well, she thinks. The floors were ruined by the mice, anyway.

J.C. falls into a deep sleep. In her dream, Drosselmeyer comes to visit her. She is in her bed, her arm wrapped in a length of snow white gauze. Memories of a year-long battle with serious wrist surgeries causes her unease, but when her godfather brings to her the nutcracker, she realizes she is dealing with something far stranger than orthopedic distress. The nutcracker's jaw has been rehinged, and there is no sign of the ACE bandage anywhere. J.C. expects Drosselmeyer to leave right away, what, with his busy social schedule and all, but the older man sits on the edge of the couch and begins to tell her a story about Princess Pirlipat and Madam Mouserinks — also known as the Queen of Mice — instead.

According to Drosselmeyer, The Mouse Queen was a nasty, underhanded rodent. She tricked Pirlipat's mother into allowing her and her children to eat up all the lard that was meant for the king's sausage supper. Of course, this enrages the king, and because he's angry, the queen is unhappy as well. The king, hungry and disgruntled, orders his court inventor to create traps for the Mouse Queen and her fat and well-fed children.

The inventor, who happens to share the Drosselmeyer name, does as he's asked. His traps are successful. He manages to kill all Madam Mouserinks' children, which makes her very mad indeed. She swears to take revenge on the king's daughter, Princess Pirlipat.

Pirlipat's mother, terrified that harm will come to her child, surrounds the princess with many cats. These cats like to nap, as cats are known to do, so the child's nurses are instructed to constantly stroke the felines. Unfortunately, even nurses get tired, and they—as well as the cats—fall asleep. The Mouse Queen takes advantage.

She uses magic to turn Pirlipat, who is known to be quite beautiful just as most children are, into something hideous. Her head is now enlarged. She is given a wide, grinning mouth, and from her chin sprouts a cottony beard. She resembles a nutcracker more than she does a little girl, and, understandably, this makes the king furious. He blames Drosselmeyer and gives the inventor four weeks to find a cure for his stricken daughter. When a month passes and Drosselmeyer has not come up with a way to bring Pirlipat back to herself, he begs his friend, the court astrologer, for help.

Together they read Pirlipat's horoscope and find that the only way she can be cured is if she eats a Crackatook nut. As if that isn't obscure enough, this nut must be cracked and given to her by a man who has never worn a pair of boots or taken a razor to his face in his entire life. It gets worse than that, though. This man also must hand her the nut without opening his eyes, then take seven steps backward without so much as a stumble.

I have always known finding a good man is a difficult task, but poor Pirlipat ... Not only did she have a really messed up name, but the man she was looking for? Well, I wasn't sure she was going to have any sort of luck at all finding him.

The king obviously feels the same way because he is beside himself at the news. The odds seem slim to none, but this is his little girl. He can't sit around and do nothing. Well, he can sit around and do nothing. He's the king. He finds someone to do his running around for him.

He calls Drosselmeyer and the astrologer and demands that the two of them go out and search for both the Crackatook nut and the man they need to give that nut to his daughter. The pair leave with the king's threat of a very long and painful death should they return unsuccessful.

For many years, the men travel without finding either the Crackatook or the man. During their long journey, they find themselves in Nuremburg and take shelter with Drosselmeyer's cousin who is a puppet maker. They think they have failed in their search and tell the puppet maker why they have been away from the castle for so long. Surprised, the artisan pulls from a small pouch the very Crackatook nut they have been looking for. Later, when the astrologer and the inventor meet the puppet maker's son, they realize this is the man they need to crack the nut and present it to the woefully ugly Pirlipat.

The three of them arrive at the castle, and the king is overjoyed. He tells Drosselmeyer's nephew that if he can crack the nut and give it to his daughter, he will give him Pirlipat's hand in marriage. The young man raises the Crackatook up to his bearded face, pops it into his mouth and crack! The hard shell splits open as easy as you please. He closes his eyes, hands the kernel to Pirlipat and takes seven steps backward with his bootless feet. The princess swallows the nut and presto, chango! The big head disappears. The beard vanishes, and the wide grin is replaced by a beautiful, girlish smile.

Unfortunately for Drosselmeyer's nephew, that seventh step is a doozy. His heel comes down right on top of Madame Mouserinks, the Mouse Queen, causing him to stumble. The curse that is lifted from Pirlipat then falls on him. His handsome visage changes, and he becomes the nutcracker. Although the princess is once again beautiful on the outside, her soul proves to be surprisingly ugly. Seeing the changes that have overcome her hero, Pirlipat banishes young Drosselmeyer from the castle instead of becoming his wife. She is the princess. She has options, especially now that the spell has been lifted.

How rude.

J.C.'s godfather, seeing that he has tired her out with his tale, leaves her so that she can rest. Her sleep is not deep and is colored by strange images. She blames it on the painkillers she's been given for the nasty cut on her arm, but in her dream, the visions come from another source. It's the seven headed Mouse King, and he's whispering into her ear, threatening to bite the newly mended nutcracker that stands at her bedside to pieces unless she gives him sweets … and the recipe for the cheeseball she served on Christmas Eve.

For the nutcracker's sake, she sacrifices both her candy and the recipe, but the Mouse King is a greedy liar. He continues to threaten J.C. until the nutcracker intervenes, telling her that if she will find him a sword, he will finish the seven-headed menace off once and for all. She finds a sword among the debris left when the toy cabinet fell and crashed to the floor and gives it to the nutcracker.

Let's be honest here. Even if this wasn't a dream, the mess would most likely still be there. J.C. isn't the best housekeeper, remember?

She drifts back into her restless sleep, and when she sees the nutcracker in her thoughts again, he has with him all the Mouse King's seven crowns. The hideous rodent has been conquered!

The nutcracker takes J.C. with him to the Land of Sweets where the Sugar Plum Fairy rules. They are offered chocolates from Spain, coffee from Arabia, tea from China, and candy canes from Russia. While they eat and drink, Danish shepherdesses perform on their flutes, and Mother Ginger, a rather odd looking woman, introduces them to her twenty or so offspring. There is much dancing, but J.C. feels a bit sick from the sugar and caffeine overload and begs to be taken back to her bed.

It is several days before J.C. awakens. When she looks around her home she realizes that the mess she left behind has been cleaned up. The dishes have been done and, as she suspected, there is no toy cabinet, broken or otherwise in her living room. What she cut her arm on is still a mystery, but she is sure, in time, she will figure it out.

She hears a knock on the door and opens it to find her godfather, Drosselmeyer, standing on her porch. He says he has come to fix the clock. She tells him there is no clock to fix, unless he wants to look at her microwave, but the last time she checked, that one was working just fine. Drosselmeyer brushes past her and steps inside.

Drosselmeyer tinkers with the unbroken microwave, and J.C. spies the nutcracker that is now resting upon the bookshelves. Her mind wanders to the story her godfather told her. He watches her as she lifts her hand to touch one of the nutcracker's wooden boots. He smiles and tells her that he's glad she is nothing like Pirlipat. He knows had she been in the princess's rather expensive silk shoes that she would have loved the man who had saved her no matter what he looked like. He smiles and asks her if his assessment is correct.

J.C. shrugs. Sure, she tells him. It's what's inside that counts. Besides, this question is purely hypothetical. Right?

The conversation is interrupted when Drosselmeyer's cell phone sounds from the pocket of his jacket. There is talk of an arriving flight. From where, J.C. asks. Nuremberg, her godfather responds. Who is coming to visit? It's Drosselmeyer's nephew.

J.C. cocks a disbelieving eyebrow in his direction.

She shoos him through her kitchen, down the stairs and out the front door. She tells him he best be on his way. It's a long drive to the airport. Before she shuts the door on him she gives him a smile and reminds him that she doesn't care how handsome his nephew is. She's happily married, and she has no use for his gift, the nutcracker. The only nuts she likes to eat are already shelled and come in a can.

The End

About the Author

J.C. Wing is a novelist who writes both southern lit and romantic comedy, but she's got plans to tackle a few other genres in the not too distant future. Her works include *The Color of Thunder, The Gannon Family Series* and the *Goddess of Tornado Alley Series*. She was also a contributing author for *Perfectly Unique: The Missing Pieces Anthology,* which was written to support Autism Speaks.

J.C. has a fondness for peanut M & M's, iced chai tea, Greek mythology and reading really good books. She's worked for A & H Publishing, Kids 411 Magazine and Booktrope. In 2016, she decided to work for herself and launched Wing Family Editing. She publishes under Black Cat Press, her own imprint. J.C. is part of an author collective called Hummingbird Charm where she hangs out with a group of amazing women and writes about her experiences with both homeschooling and life.

J.C. is an eternal optimist and a friendly sort. She smiles a lot ... but she is silently correcting your grammar. She doesn't mean to. She's an editor. She can't help it.

72820254R00084

Made in the USA
Middletown, DE
09 May 2018